Queen of Tarts

by

L. J. Greatrex

Acknowledgements

The writing of this book has only been achieved with the continued support and love of my family and friends.

Many thanks also to Darin Jewell, my literary agent from The Inspira Group, who has worked patiently and professionally in the publication of my books.

Preface

It's well-known that every high school has one and Jessica Turner was no exception. Always first to flirt or smile sweetly over her shoulder, her prey didn't stand a chance.

Far from being the shrinking violet her mother had expected due to her uneven teeth, bedraggled hair, and essential glasses, nothing, it seemed, as she reached puberty, was unable to stop her from changing the image.

Tinted contact lenses and dentist appointments proved a vital part of her transformation.

The bill, eye-watering for teeth straightening and whitening, added to the optician's and hairdresser's hefty monthly account, her father was astounded.

Jessica, now shortened to Jess, was in a bid to change the perception she was destined to be a swot on the shelf indefinitely and to discourage any idea she would stay in the shadows a moment longer.

Long-suffering as a child growing up with tall, good-looking, long-legged, brunette siblings, Jess's mousey hair that was now vibrant red was her first statement.

Although she could do nothing to heighten her stance, her voluptuous breasts, her most outstanding attribute, were used to their best advantage.

Wolf whistles, exchanged for a slap on the back for a good sort, Jess was more determined than ever never to look back on those woeful days.

Asked to carry her document case instead of being piled high with sweaty baseball shirts expected to be returned to the laundry room, her days of falling foul of any boy's derogatory sexism, whether intended or not, was over, full stop.

"It only takes a moment," Jess's vocal talents added to by her voice coach, another expense in a long line of extravagancies her father despaired of when he finally realised her intention.

Her mom insisted that it was growing pains and she would soon be back to 'normal' (whatever normal was) now that she had the bull by the horns. Jess, her youngest and brightest, had no intention of returning to the wilting lily, as her reputation as a good catch flew through the corridors of high school at a rate of knots.

The summer of 1960 saw the beginning of a revolution of changed attitudes. Jess laughed as she heard the term sex, drugs and rock n roll. She intended to try them all.

Well, perhaps excluding the drugs. Her education as to the dangers of such practices rang in her ears, "These are only for the new generation superstars and not the likes of the more level-headed." Her mom's forever sensible quotes and the lack of funds kept Jess mostly on the straight and narrow.

These were heady days, dancing each night, resting only on Sunday in time to recover for the office the next morning. Life was good.

So much lay ahead and despite many offers of 'friends with benefits', Jess had better fish to fry.

No intention of being labelled easy, Jess made a decision that painted nails were better than dishpan hands and a coiffeur far superior to a shampoo and set.

Saving for designer labels in preference to off-the-peg, fewer garments, but better statements were her ideals.

Taking a second look at her image in the dressing room mirror, Jess was almost satisfied she had met her goal.

Looking seriously like a film star, speaking with an accent more suited to gentry and singing voice to put Maria Callas in the shade, now all she needed was a wealthy arm to lean upon.

Chapter One

It was November and all but a few of the leaves had fallen from the trees. Hats, coats, mufflers and boots were the everyday garb now that the wind had changed for the worst.

Not so for Jess. The warm log fire burning in the hearth of the most prestigious hotel in New York was setting the scene.

Standing sipping champagne, checking the occupancy for rich and available men, no divorced or pretending to be for Jess, her man must be the real 'McCoy'.

The challenge, Jess soon discovered, was sorting through which was which!

Destined to be hoodwinked, or so her suitors thought, her selection began.

With too many gigolos and pretend singles for Jess's liking, she turned to the Forbes directory as guidance for her requirements.

Not the old-fashioned love as most girls her age seek, hers was a more modern approach. To enable love to last (in Jess's opinion), her choice of spouse would have to fall into certain categories.

Firstly, rich enough to keep her in a way that would enable her to live in luxury. Second, to be presentable enough to satisfy her not only in bed, but on the entertainment and party scene.

She wasn't averse to an older, more experienced candidate. This would take her one more step closer to having wealth in her own right.

Preferably an investment guru or oil-rich man, slightly naive, good looking, but not so much so that he was the target of all and-sundry females.

Jess coveted a more respectable but party-loving way of life without the drudge her contemporaries unwittingly fell into.

Not too much to ask, she convinced herself, posing but not too obvious, hoping to catch the man of her dreams.

The fireplace in the high-end hotel was a perfect place on a New Year's Eve to select her prey.

The Texas drawl of Mark Burnettie, the first to catch Jess's eye, seemed to fit the bill, although a disappointment to begin with. Not a shrinking violet, more a man of the world, he ticked most of the boxes but not all.

Undeterred due to his obscene wealth, Jessica, her recently reverted to name, decided to give him more time to prove his suitability.

"Your father left you his entire estate?" her question loaded.

"Forget it! If you think I fall for the first line that tumbles from a woman's lips, you are sorely mistaken," his gold tooth glistened as he grinned his knowledge of a gold digger, or 'oil well' in his case when he set eyes on one.

"My, my, we do have a low opinion of the fairer sex. Which python bit your fanny?" She laughed, turning to move on.

The look of surprise at her quick retort surprised him, not having encountered such a brash rebuttal before.

Mark, more used to pandering, said, "You amuse me." Her plan to shock was working. "What brings you to New York if not to net yourself a husband?"

"Thanks for the offer," Jess laughed, "but you're not my type." She turned to leave.

"And what, may I ask, is your type, as you put it?" Mark the 'mark', questioned, now curious as to her preference.

"Certainly not an up-himself Texan with no manners," her comment aimed at his unsuitability as even a conversation piece.

"Wow, you know how to put a man down," he replied, awaiting her retaliation.

"If you're looking for a boost to your ego, look elsewhere." Jess began conversing with a woman in her forties, equally elegant in her Versace gown.

Keeping one eye on her Texan, Jess followed the crowd into the dining area. Having checked the guest list and selected Mark for her attention, she was not surprised the two sat alongside.

"We meet again," Mark said, sitting uncomfortably in the next chair.

"Promise you won't bite me. I'm allergic to venom," she murmured out of earshot of the surrounding company.

"There you go again, calling me a snake when you have no idea who I am." Mark was unable to believe this good-looking creature could hand out more insults in one hour than he had experienced in his lifetime.

"You presumed me to be a gold digger, if I recall correctly, when you also have no idea who I am."

"Touché," Mark whispered, followed by, "Is it possible to start again since we are destined to share each other's company throughout the meal?"

"Only if you promise not to harass me," Jess inwardly smiled. He had taken the bait.

"Long time no see!" The outstretched hand gave way for Jess to decide to either pretend she hadn't seen him or place a kiss on his mouth to shut him up.

"William, so pleased to see you. How come you're slumming with the rest of the riffraff?" was the best she could come up with, drawing his attention to the company of the mega-rich.

"This way," she took him to one side. "I'm with someone and he's awfully jealous. Can we meet later?" She handed him a card supposedly containing her room number. She smiled sweetly. "Great to see you again. Give my love to the count," Jess called out in earshot of Mark.

William, Bill as she knew him, nodded with a look of complete confusion, "What?" He began to speak before Jess scooted him with her hand.

"Another admirer?" Mark smiled a knowing smile.

"He's way above your league," she lifted her nose.

"You have no idea what my league is!" Mark replied, indignant with her assumption.

"And have no desire to!" Still cutting edge, she walked across the dance floor and onto the unsuspecting arm of a stranger.

"Please, will you dance with me? I have an unwanted admirer." She smiled her practiced little girl lost smile.

"My pleasure," Archibald, Archie for short, whisked her onto the dance floor. "Do you come here often?" the old adage seeming corny. Jess laughed.

"Only in the mating season!" Jessica retorted, holding her breath as his pale blue eyes and perfectly coiffured blond hair caught her attention.

"I'm happy to oblige on both counts!" His cheeky grin was fascinating.

"Hmm, you have possibilities," she looked him up and down. "Are you married?" the question left hanging.

"Only if you're asking." He liked this woman.

"Before we get carried away, I'm Jessica, Jess for short." The thought of what Mark thought or didn't think completely left her mind.

"I'm Archibald, Archie for short." He couldn't help smiling. This was one hell-of-a smooth operator. "Where are you from?"

"Where do you want me to be from?" Jess smiled with her rehearsed 'pretty woman' look.

"I know where I want you to end up!" He laughed a sexy laugh.

"Maybe we're on the same wavelength after all!" Jess equalled his sexy stare.

"Your room or mine?" he added, well and truly hooked on this vision of loveliness.

No more said, he took her hand and she disappeared from Mark's sight.

The suite just below the penthouse was inviting. Before she could compliment him on his taste, he had his jacket and bow tie off and began removing her gown.

"Down boy, you haven't asked permission!" Jess said, holding tight to her modesty.

He went down on one knee. "Will you marry me?" he smiled an urgent smile.

"I don't know you, nor you me. Get up, you fool. Before I marry or sleep with anyone, they must meet my criteria."

"And that is? If I don't have it, I'll get it. Whatever it is," he added, his tone gruff with anticipation.

Jess broke into fits of laughter, "You're surely the most arrogant suitor I have ever had. Are you always so forthright?"

"You bring out the animal in me!" he answered, hoping to achieve her consent.

Jess turned and swiftly walked to the door. No man, no matter their favourable banter, would trick her into bed.

Archie sat looking at the closed door crestfallen. Despite his marital status, his good looks and easy banter had always achieved his goal before. "You'll be back!" he called after her, angry his technique, or lack of it, hadn't worked.

Back to Mark with a sweet smile and a toss of the head, "Have you missed me?" Jess laughed. He looked bewildered, drinking his fourth martini.

Most men drifted to the bar for a glass of port, a cigar and a game of cards, but not Mark. His suggestion he was not partial to the normal male pursuits caused her to question his preferences.

Clarifying his position, he described being caught many times before by professional gamblers, who thought him an easy target.

Politely easing herself onto a high stool at the bar, Mark's expectation Jess would run up his tab was surprised when Jess politely refused. "I'm not easily bought by a few glasses of wine," she laughed spritely, nodding to the barman as pre-arranged.

A wine glass of water between each glass of chardonnay had been explained to the barman as necessary due to her not wishing to fall foul of male advances, as was the same reason for having her own tab.

Jess had to save for months before putting this practice in place, but necessary due to most rich men feeling a few drinks paid for equalled a 'tart'.

Chapter Two

So far, so good. Jess hoped her night and her savings had not been wasted. The fact that this was the first of hopefully not many attempts to net her a husband, her cash flow determined how many times every six months she was able to try.

Staying within spying distance of Mark's position, she smiled on her way to the ladies' room. Just long enough, but not too long for him to get bored and leave. She powdered her nose and returned to his chosen place.

Without a second glance, a hand holding a glass of champagne appeared from nowhere. "Get lost," the brunette whispered out of Mark's hearing.

Without recognition of the command, Jess lifted her arm and the champagne washed down the front of the intruder's bosom.

"Oh dear, so sorry, let me help you!" Pushing the brunette toward the powder room, Jess held tight to her arm. "I'm his wife, you evil bitch. If you want to keep your looks, you better scarper quick!"

To say the brunette was put in her place was an understatement. Wiping herself down, she disappeared without a trace.

"Mark, sorry to have disturbed your tête-à-tête. I hope I didn't spoil her new dress?" Jess said sarcastically. Mark shook his head as if he hadn't noticed.

"Where were we?" Jess added, a perfect set of teeth on display.

"I'm not sure we were anywhere. I thought you had better fish to fry." Mark looked suitably unimpressed.

"What makes you think that?" she answered, smiling.

Feeling out of his depth with her new stance, Mark didn't answer.

"The shark you were entertaining gave me the impression she had some sort of hold over you."

"I hadn't seen her before. Why, what did she say?"

"That you were pestering her!" Jess lied.

"I have no need to pester anyone." Mark emptied his glass.

"Hmm, I guessed that. Must be her inferiority complex. Something I have no need of," Jess reeling him in, replied.

"Why, if you have an aversion to me, do you continue to stand there?" Mark, now curious as to her reasoning, remarked.

"I stand where I wish. If you're upset by my presence, move on!" Jess turned to face the other way.

"OK, I get it. You like to play games!" Mark said, out of his depth with such arrogance.

"Why would I need to? I don't play games with self-important males on an ego trip!" Jess replied, trying to provoke him. Just enough to keep his curiosity, but not too much to scare him off.

"It appears another new start is needed here!" Mark tired of her insults, conceded.

"Maybe so." Jess felt satisfied she had him in her palm and changed her disposition.

"I'm Jessica Turner," Jess smiled a compelling smile.

"I'm Mark Burnettie," he returned her smile.

The evening progressed and they discussed anything but their financial standing or expectations of future mates.

Jess had no need. Forbes directory told her everything she needed to know.

Surprised by his intelligence, Mark equally so of her worldliness, his offer of a second date was exactly as Jess had manoeuvred. Her answer, considering her manner to begin with, shocked him.

Feeling uncertain of her acceptance for many reasons, one being her lack of interest in his financial status, he waited with bated breath.

"I would like to see you again," Jess's smile this time partly genuine.

Is it possible a man of such wealth could also be a normal human being? A question as to her misconception hung heavy in her mind. He hailed a taxi for her as his chauffeur awaited his presence.

No 'come up and see my penthouse', as she had expected. The assumption she would prefer to make her own assessment of his suitability following more than one encounter was a first for Jess.

Unbeknownst to Mark, she already knew everything a girl like her needed to know. Not only of his wealth but his family, his many mansions throughout the world and most of all, what lay behind the mask of one of the most respected men in Texas.

Jess was a little apprehensive she had bitten off more than she could chew on this occasion.

She thought he was a typical wealthy playboy, despite his reputation in the business world, with money to burn and time on his hands to do with as he wished, with whom he wished.

She lay thinking of the evening. Not of William, who almost gave the show away, or Archie, the obvious out-for-what-he-could-get gigolo. It was time to assess her progress with Mark, mostly due to no invitation to come up for a drink. The typical response to satisfy most male egos, Jess wondered if the call promised would materialise.

Mark was a little taken aback. The usual offer of sex before a trap hadn't been mentioned. Could his first opinion of this unusual girl have been wrong?

His biggest surprise, his normal reaction to such blatant put-downs, hers had caused a stir in him long since smothered by countless parasites out for a financial score. He spent the night setting the scene for a further encounter.

Unable to concentrate on his normal level, the run through the grounds of his mansion used mostly to think through business deals or investments was constantly interrupted by his thoughts of Jessica.

What is it that drew her to him? He was a loner with very little time for entertaining or being entertained. The New Year invitation to the hotel where they met was only taken up due to the coming election of a new president and his closest friend's request for donations.

It wasn't as if he had been seduced into suggesting a second meeting. Far from it, he had received more insults from the time he set eyes on her than in his whole life.

Mostly, women made it obvious they were attracted not to his good looks or charisma but to his position and wealth. It shocked Mark to think this had not been the case with this infuriating but fascinating young woman.

"This is nice!" Her response to one of the most prestigious restaurants in the city, set him thinking Jessica was accustomed to better.

"The food is extremely good and their wine seller is next to none," Mark said, thinking he had to justify his choice of venue.

"I'm sure you're right," Jess left it there as the manager greeted Mark with familiarity.

Holding her seat, the waiter smiled, "Is madam happy with the choice of table?"

"It's fine," Jess's reply was not gushing like others Mark had entertained, other than his mother's matchmaking friends' daughters.

Jess's after school education had been added to by a reconnaissance of not only the best hotels and restaurants, but everything that the wealthy naturally took for granted.

Honed to perfection for her purpose, the food on the French menu read with ease to order with no hesitation as to her choice.

Jess read the wine list as if she had written it herself. Her favourites reeled off as the glass to be sniffed and sipped was hastily rejected until the perfect wine was chosen for the dish.

"A connoisseur?" Mark, surprised by her skill, questioned.

Jess laughed as if it were a flippant question, "Let's say, I have tasted wines that suit most meals."

Giving nothing away without lying, she had certainly drunk lots of wine, but not of this calibre. Her drink with food from takeaways was substandard by comparison to the cuisine served, but Jess felt sure her future needs would be met by her mega-rich host.

Jess recollected from Mark's father's memoirs that he was the only son of a Texas inheritor.

A distant family prospector finding oil by accident on land claimed alongside his wife was Mark's eventual benefactor. After months of travelling over hundreds of miles of rough terrain with others less fortunate, his ancestor had reaped benefits beyond his wildest dreams.

They had settled, thinking cattle was their goal, until one morning, whilst sinking a well for water, it turned black and began spilling out all over their grazing land, gushing higher than the barn Mark's past generation had sweated to erect for their cows.

The shock expressed in the book as his distant relative realised his good fortune was described with passion and detail even Jess could relate to.

Nothing left to chance, her reading and inwardly digesting for a later date, her fascination with Mark's history not only of their wealth but tenacity and sacrifice, the likes of which she had little knowledge.

Her awareness of his family's achievements was hidden as he explained his history without embellishment.

Giving nothing away as to the extent of his wealth, Mark did not wish to encourage her attention for reasons other than her feelings for him as a man and not a bank account, so he tried to lessen his outward persona.

Coincidentally, Jess laid the groundwork for an increase in her family's lack of good fortune by pretending to be better placed in the money stakes than she was.

This was difficult as time passed as a genuine feeling of well-being in his presence took over from her planned indifference.

A secure future, being spoilt, spending her days sunning herself by day and dancing under the stars by night. *What more could a girl want?* Jess asked herself.

She soon realised Mark worked hard and spent most days keeping his fortune in place, not just for himself but for all the people who relied upon him for their livelihood.

This was a side she admired, but one she hadn't considered the rich embarked upon.

A boardroom full of people keeping the cash flowing whilst the owner whiled his way through life being waited on hand and foot was her thinking. Flying all over the world at the drop of a hat on his jet to anywhere in the world that took his fancy had been her expectation.

This was just a pipe dream and Jess soon realised it. The only problem was that she was growing fond of her multi-billionaire. Not something she had factored into her situation.

The more he wined and dined her and the more her feelings were reciprocated by Mark, the more difficult her position became.

Money, no object, ticked her first box. Waiting each day for his call, either saying he would be late or not turning up at all, was far from her ideal.

The draw of this man, not just physically but emotionally, was a disaster to her original expectations.

"Please, can you find time for holiday? I'm lonely and need you," Jess found herself pleading, having realised her original perception was far off mark.

"Sorry, darling, this is not easy for me either. I wish things were different," Mark said, having made love to her twice before leaving for the office.

Jess's plan to leave her family behind finally got the better of her. "Hi, Mom, are you in today?" Her call sounded pleading.

"Of course, darling, are you ok? You sound strange," her mom said, thinking Jess was away most of the time, having the time of her life, and hadn't thought her absence unusual.

Partly explaining her dilemma, Jess felt trapped between the life she had hoped for and the life she now shared with Mark.

Not a marriage made in heaven with a man totally besotted by her, taking her all over the world. The singing and dancing lessons in mothballs, her daily shopping trips as his mistress expected to fill the gap in her humdrum life was no compensation for her expectations.

Jess was about to re-evaluate her situation when the bubble burst.

"I need to see you now!" The phone call to meet Mark in a pavement café was not the answer to her disillusionment but more a command. "You lied to me. You're no better than a streetwalker. Just better dressed at my expense.

"No need for more lies. Pack your bag. You can take all the trappings you conned me out of and be gone before I get home." The anxiety in his eyes as they welled with tears rendered Jess to despair.

Unable to justify her deception despite her feelings of love for him now, Jess sat mortified. Not for the loss of the fortune he spent on her, as would have been her previous requisite, but the strong and enduring love grown over the time they spent together.

"Is there nothing I can say?" Jess questioned as the whole sorry story spilled out.

"Nothing!" Mark shouted. "You can keep the engagement ring. Sell it, it will see your greed through the next months." He sent the ring flying back in her direction.

"Mark, I love you!" Jess pleaded, but her pleas fell on deaf ears.

Chapter Three

Months past, all communication denied, Jess realised deceit had changed her life forever.

Had she not been made aware in a five-page letter from Mark how he stumbled over her deception, there may have been a slim chance to retrieve the love they'd shared.

His bumping into William in a men's club had been her Achilles heel. Descriptive in every detail, he left nothing unsaid regarding Jess's wealth creation scheme.

Embellished to hurt due to her dismissing him with a flick of her hand, William sealed her fate from the onset.

The affair she and William shared with a passion given freely was centre stage.

Jess's background, early disadvantages, her unusual appearance before the transformation had been aired like washing on a line.

Having known William (Bill) back then, his rendition related the whole sorry tale. His bitter story, driven by revenge following her rebuttal, left nothing out.

Had Mark given her time to explain she had changed due to the love she now felt, the outcome may have been different.

Although Jess thought as she sat broken-hearted, had her desperate need to live the high life without all the challenges her humble beginnings afforded, maybe her life wouldn't be in ruins now.

Her tears wetting the pages, she blamed herself as Mark spelled out his loathing. What was difficult to understand was why William would go to such lengths to give her no recourse. Maybe the adage 'Hell hath no fury like a woman scorned' applied to males as well.

Not wanting to go back to her humble beginnings or feel the hurt of real love, Jess pledged never to let anyone get close or anything stand in her way again.

The large house on the corner of Consequence Avenue was chosen not only as a distraction to the feelings she still harboured for Mark, but also to avail her the financial stability needed to fulfil her future needs.

The engagement ring, worth far more than Jess first thought, had been sold, although she'd spent hours wearing it, crying, hoping he would find it in his heart to forgive her. This was now her only way out.

Empty and neglected, Jess made up her mind once the renovations had been made, she'd have a perfect venue for earning a living.

Despite its outward appearance, creepers and stems left to grow through every crevice and floorboard, Jess's fascination with all things rustic grew with her curiosity.

Wiping a window with her sleeve, breathing heavily to clear a small spy hole, enough to see the old fireplace with its marble façade was everything the outside confirmed. This was the place she could make her own.

Holding her breath, she made her way down an overgrown path leading to a broken-down gate. Pushing hard as the hinges creaked and the stubborn weeds refused to budge, it would need a miracle to fix the garden behind if this was an example.

Better left to the vermin and birds, it was obvious nothing short of a military operation would bring the jungle behind back to life.

Jess was more determined than ever that her hasty purchase would work, which it had to, considering every penny she'd saved alongside Mark's generous nature had got her this far.

Undaunted as the gate screeched open just enough to squeeze through, the surprise of a lovely, although overgrown garden, spread out before her.

Open-mouthed, she gazed at the expanse: a fountain, an orchard cultivated to form an arch, wildflowers of every colour and description. Jess sat in the middle and cried

French lessons would surely lead to a steady income. Maybe her talent for refinement, posture and how to conduct herself socially, learned when seeking a rich husband, would be the answer.

Not on the grand scale of a Swiss finishing school, but a more modest approach would be advertised to attract a clientele able to pay.

Interviewing a stream of architects, builders, carpenters, painters and gardeners kept Jess occupied during her transition from tart to mistress of her own fate.

Nothing in her chosen distraction could compensate her feelings of desolation as she thought of Mark. If Jess had learned anything, it was to never repeat the same sorry story again.

A path to riches and love on hold indefinitely, hard work and building something worthwhile was Jess's new mantra.

The years spent engineering a future reliant on a man were over. It was time to steer her direction into creating a new life, forced once again by circumstance.

Using her skills learned to guarantee what she had with Mark, from a home she'd gladly left behind, Jess planned each stage along the way.

Instructions to her chosen architect not to change the outward appearance other than cosmetic, her feelings of a once-loved home were strong as she wandered around.

The inside impression was of grandeur despite the cobwebs. The staircase stirred her, thinking of ladies from the past, floating in gowns of taffeta, silk and satin, downwards to a party in the elegant ballroom. Her imagination ran riot.

There were goose bumps down her spine as she pictured the scene of dancers holding each other, the music, the...... Jess began crying uncontrollably as the thought of Mark and the scent of him filled her thoughts.

"No more," she chastised herself, blowing dust from a mirror. "Those are the last tears I shed over any man," she cried aloud, seeing a reflection she hardly recognised.

Looking up, wiping the last vestige of tears from her cheeks, Jess spotted a guy trying to wend his way through the brambles.

"Beg pardon, missy, I wondered where the mistress was. I have to see her about the orchard."

"That's me," Jess answered, brushing dust from her hair. "I'll just be a minute!"

Walking to the study, or so-called until she could perfect it, she collected her notes. Everything had been learned that could be about the garden, plants, lawns, soil, and trees and which pruning suited which was instilled in her memory.

The young man stood rolling his hat in a fashion reminding Jess of her father. Although his stature was of a young, attractive male, his behaviour was more of a gentle adolescent. "This way. I have grand hopes for the fruit. There are many types," Jess directed with her hand towards the pear trees. "These are my favourite. I hope you can bring them to bear fruit once more. They've been sadly neglected, I'm sorry to say." Jess smiled.

"I'll get started right away. I have a liking for all fruit and what helps them grow," Howard nodded as he walked along, taking notes.

"I'll order whatever you suggest. You come highly recommended from many in the village," she added with a smile. Not the smile intended to catch a rich mate, just a regular smile she had practised for all occasions.

"That's good to know," Howard bowed slightly from the neck. "As soon as I'm finished, I'll let you have a list of what is needed." Looking toward the path between the rows of different fruit, he began checking the leaves for aphids.

She felt happy Howard would meet her requirements despite his slightly unusual manner. Should he have been more assertive and less like someone much younger, he would fit the bill as a stud.

Jess chastised herself. That would have been her old thinking, not the newly invented businesswoman of intellect and style.

He strolled around the building, adding to Jess's drawings with some things agreed upon and removing impracticalities of others. "Ms Turner, I have completed the survey. Most of your suggestions marry with my own. Some I have taken account of, and others need later discussion. I have amended where necessary based on local planning regulations."

"Thank you! May I call you John?" Jess smiled, adding, "Please call me Jess. I look forward to seeing

31

your first draft. I`m sure our combined ideas will be sympathetic to the property's era.

"The alterations inside are for necessity due to my business interests. These I wish carried out with the same consideration and sympathy." Jess turned to her list of priorities.

Pointing to the ceiling, demonstrating the cornice with her hand, Jess moved along indicating the need for restoration.

"I will take great care to portray your requests to the builders. It is my normal practise to meet on a regular basis with my clients and the builders to confirm their agreement."

"Thank you, John, we appear to be singing from the same hymn sheet," Jess said, happy she had chosen well.

It would take some time for John to get back to her for their first meeting. In the meantime, Jess settled herself the best she could into two rooms. One room to sleep in and store the remainder of the clothes purchased for her by Mark. The others were sold, including a mink coat, to raise additional funds for the project.

The second room was a section to the end of the large rambling kitchen, complete with an ancient stove still hosting a variety of implements Jess didn't recognise.

It crossed her mind that not only would this suit her purpose in the short team for storing food and a place to eat, but these artifacts would be ideal as a statement from the past to be handed down to ladies of more modern days as an insight into a bygone age.

Jess did her best to remain positive. Not easy at present in the squalid circumstances and with bills arriving at a rate of knots.

Talking to herself, as visitors were scant, she said, "I may need investors." Her conclusion, based on the spiralling costs, forced her to think of the rich she had met during her time with Mark.

Not for the same reason as before her change of heart and not one of his close friends, as they may be tempted to tell him of her plans. Jess made a list as far as she recalled. One or two rich people she met during her time with Mark would meet her criterion.

Archie the letch, although he was listed in the top ten, was ruled out without question. William crossed out with vengeance due to his betrayal. Many other acquaintances faded with time, her only other memory was of a lady she turned to as a ploy to reign in Mark.

The diamond necklace and a gown designed by Gianni Versace to die for was hard to forget.

Recalling their conversation, the woman had introduced herself as Julia Weinbergen from Michigan or Ohio. The lakeside mansion she described verbally seemed perfect for the very rich.

She turned once more to the Forbes. "Hmm… Weinbergen, Julia." Her family was well up the rich list. Jess took the bull by the horns and made the call.

"Hi, is Julia Weinbergen in? It's Jessica Turner."

"Sorry, she's out at present. Can I ask her to call you back?" a very official sounding voice, obviously her secretary, asked.

Giving the telephone number recently installed into her shambles, Jess hoped Julia would remember their encounter.

There were many high-end associates of Mark's introduced to her during their time together, but only a few impressed her enough to qualify as possible partners in her new venture.

Although to Jess, any person investing in her project would only be considered a sleeping partner. She wanted no interference in an operation inspired by her own qualities and aspirations.

Chapter Four

This was another journey carefully mapped to include not only someone with money and similar objectives, but without the customary male influence.

"Ms Weinbergen, I hope this isn't an imposition," Jess began, having had a call back. "You may recall we met at last New Year's Eve party. I was accompanied by Mark Burnettie." Name dropping for effect, Jess awaited her recollection.

"Of course. Jessica, isn't it?" she hesitated. "It was a wonderful evening. We must do it again soon."

Hoping her enthusiasm didn't resonate in her voice, Jess said, "I agree. That's why I'm calling. Can we meet somewhere? I have a proposition for you." Jess thought straight talk with people of standing would pave the way for success. Although Jess couldn't remember who said it, it was a reasonable assumption.

"It sounds intriguing," Jess heard rustling. "I have next Wednesday if that's ok. Maybe twelve o-clock at the Ivy?"

"That would be great. I'll look forward to it." Jess ended the call with a smile on her face.

Writing a business plan to end all business plans needed to wet Julia's appetite, Jess, having researched the Weinbergen family, discovered her to be entrepreneurial with fingers in many pies.

A woman of so many facets would bring experience to her project. Jess was satisfied that her decision, should she agree, would pay dividends.

Investments in design, not only in fashion but a selection based on other interests, one being architecture, had figured highly in Julia's family's rise to fame and fortune. Jess was amazed by her listed talents.

Potentially, helping with the design of her project, Jess considered 'an after-college learning establishment for rich females' would whet Julia's appetite.

Daydreaming, Jess pictured her future. Further than her eye could see, through the deteriorating façade, she dreamt of her grand house fully restored.

'J & J Foundation for discerning females' would be born of a need to satisfy Jess's independence and, hopefully, Julia's desire to enhance her bottom line

"Well, what do you think?" Jess could hardly contain her excitement.

"It has possibilities. I will get my lawyer and bank manager to go over the details and get back to you." Jess, the smile on her face a first for some time, regarded Julia with affection.

Although giving nothing away as to her intention, Julia's natural talent for realising a good thing when she saw one heightened.

"I think you and I would make good bedfellows in business," Jess concluded, shaking her hand, feeling satisfied she had done everything she could to persuade Julia to join her.

Driving away in her sparkling limousine, Julia seemed her fairy godmother with all the trappings Jess hoped to acquire in the not-too-distant future.

Returning to the study, Jess settled in for the long haul of researching architectural history and was lost in a world unknown to her before.

As usual, her imagination ran away, picturing the ancestral occupants in their finery, the men in portraits still hanging along the staircase, giving rise to her vision of grandeur and posturing. Ladies in gowns more in keeping with royalty, Jess got carried away with the potential splendour of it all.

"If only they could come back and advise on the finer points of the home they shared as it stood all those years ago," Jess murmured aloud.

The cloth used for drapes and carpets unable to be restored would be last in a very long list of priorities.

More urgent were the windows and doors broken by idiots trying to enter the property. Jess was grateful they hadn't succeeded.

Not forgetting the rotting floorboards on the frontal veranda and repairs needed to leaks in the roof, it took time to record every detail, but Jess was determined to leave no stone unturned.

The bathrooms and bedrooms held their own challenges, such as roll top baths brown around taps that had dripped for years.

Four-poster beds had drapes hanging in ribbons and bedcovers hosting vermin of all denominations.

Underneath the beds, the carpet was bright. The colours able to be replicated in the restoration gave her hope.

On her knees groping, her hand found a silk scarf, a mouse trap and a gold-rimmed crock pot with a broken handle. "I know what that was used for," Jess laughed, remembering her mom's reminiscing.

Grinning at what her mother would say if she could see her now, Jess's decision was made. An area in the great hall would be used to house memorabilia of the mansion's past splendour.

Collecting and sorting as many antiques as she could carry, she admired her selection the more she discovered. It was exactly as Jess had in mind.

The challenge: a section to be cordoned off to hold the artifacts was far too small. With her idea of turning it into an almost museum, Jess wondered if selling some of them to raise money for the project would be a better idea.

She lifted the telephone. "Hi, I wonder if you could give me a valuation? I have inherited several pieces I think may be of interest." The call to the local auction house hopefully would add to her dwindling bank balance.

Without hesitation, the head valuer, Robert Walker, replied, "When can I call round?"

"As soon as. I am in the process of completing an inventory." Wanting to sound professionally aware, Jess awaited his reply.

"Will tomorrow about eleven be ok?"

Checking her empty diary, *Hope springs eternal,* Jess thought, not having had anyone visit it in an age. "Fine, I'll look forward to it."

The moment Jess put down the phone, she realised what a gigantic job it would be.

Only halfway through the house, it would be impossible to carry all of the items down the stairs and log them in time. The loft, she was sure, would house more treasures was yet to be explored.

Thinking on her feet, a talent learned when seeking a husband, Mark crossed her mind for a moment. *He would think me stupid. More big ideas to crumble around my ears.*

Jess closed her thoughts to the past. It would take some time and lots of resilience to make him disappear completely.

Changing her thoughts to include Robert Walker, Jess balanced a heavy cut glass vase down the stairs. Even Jess knew this piece was valuable. The weight and images of the family cut into the glass was a sight to behold.

Thinking of hiring professionals for the heavy work, the inventory left to the valuers, Jess glanced at her at nails full of dirt and hands better sported by janitors. "Look and weep!" she whispered to herself, thinking of days forced to the back of her mind.

The problem with Jess's ideas of grandeur was her inability to pay. Before the auction could be arranged, she would need dollars to cover the costs.

A walk through the garden to refresh her thoughts, she was surprised by Howard. "Sorry, missy, I was concentrating as to the colour of the geraniums needed to complete the inner circle of the fountain," he stuttered.

"Please call me Jess. It's much less formal!" she smiled assurance this would be ok.

"Jess!" Howard practiced his new employer's name. "I have the list I promised of the needs for the orchard." He searched for the paper he had hastily tucked in his pocket.

Straightening it out with care, Howard handed it gingerly to Jess. "You will find everything in order… Jess!" it sounded strange to refer to his betters by their first name.

Smiling, Jess realised Howard had been raised by parents determined to instil respect into their teachings.

Something to note for the future with her students. Not so much bowing and scraping, but more a respectful approach towards others. *Empathy and respect*, Jess thought to herself.

The doorbell rang and Jess hid behind the curtains, thinking it a bailiff. Following many final demands for money she had run out of, Jess's heartbeat rang in her ears.

Promises not kept, withdrawal of builders until she came up with the dollars, was a nightmare unable to be unravelled until either Julia made her decision or Robert the valuer realised the revenue for the antiques.

At the sight of the limousine, as Julia stepped out accompanied by two very distinguished gents, Jess took an inward gasp. Dusting herself down, pushing her hands through her hair, she opened the door.

"Julia, what a nice surprise!" Jess hoped her racing heart was unseen through her T shirt. "Please come in. Excuse the mess. I'm just making coffee. Can I interest you and your friends?"

Trying not to ramble, her red face was a dead giveaway that she was embarrassed. No nail varnish, no make-up, hair enough to scare a crow, opposite to the image Jessica wanted to portray, a dust-ridden guise, she stood before them.

"No coffee, thanks. We are here on business," number one gent with a briefcase said as Julia stepped forward to greet her.

Julia looked around seeing no workmen in or outside of the building. "How's the project going? Well, I hope?"

"Waiting for the inspectors," Jess lied. "It would seem they are extremely busy."

"Always a problem," Julia commiserated as gent number two held out a hand.

"Andrew Marsden at your service!" He took Jess's mess-covered hand gingerly, looked down as if to kiss, changed his mind and smiled. "Keeping busy I see."

41

"Always," Jess smiled back, thinking him good looking. She wiped her hands down her jeans.

"It's probably more comfortable in here," Jess guided with her hand to the spacious dining room with a few cardboard boxes and a small card table left from the previous owners.

Julia began to laugh, "I love it when people don't put on airs and graces."

A put down to most, but Jess took it in good humour due to her need for the cash.

Julia was dressed in designer from head to toe, sitting on a crate left by plasterers. Jess's face began to relax, "Sorry, Julia, had I have known…"

Before she could utter another word, Julia lifted a perfectly manicured hand, "It's fine, really, you should see me on site sometimes. No good being a builder's daughter if you don't get your hands dirty from time to time." She smiled a genuine smile, covering her elegance faux pas.

From that moment on, the two sat discussing the pros and cons of her progress or lack of it as Julia had spotted the instant she arrived.

Andrew Marsden and Peter Deverell perched on pallets left by delivery men, listened fascinated as they were ignored in preference for two women engrossed in the intricacies of the building industry.

They reviewed the architects' plans, sorting materials to be used until the minutest detail was agreed. With the sensitive nature of the outside architecture and the finishing touches inside that Jess hoped for, Julia nodded her approval each time with enthusiasm.

"I have gardeners with many years of experience. They will keep your man...?" Julia looked around the vast expanse of wilderness, hoping it would be landscaped to perfection.

"Howard," Jess interrupted.

"More hands to the pump!" Julia smiled broader the more the discussions progressed.

Jess, delighted Howard would be trained at the same time as doing the donkey work, replied, "I'm sure he'd be happy for the extra help and the experience."

Smiling broadly, her sparkling white teeth unable to be disguised, "We're going to get on famously," Julia gushed, writing a cheque for four hundred thousand dollars. "Will that do for a start?"

Jess, unable to speak, tried hard to concentrate on the bank draft in her grubby hand. "Yes, that's fine." Fine! That's bloody marvellous, she wanted to shout.

Stretching his fingers, which clicked with the strain, Andrew, the lawyer, said, "Now for the niceties!" He smiled, lifting paperwork from his briefcase.

"Don't sign now. Have your lawyer check out the details. I'm sure he will see Andrew and Peter have covered everything. Fifty, fifty, straight down the line," Julia added, shaking Jess's hand for confirmation.

This time, no questions asked, Julia was everything Jess could wish for. Just a nod of the head and the deal was done.

Chapter Five

Taking care to log every receipt paid from Julia's investment, Jess decided applicants must meet a strict criterion. Reading a list from the agency, some young, some old, some male, some female, it seemed the world and his wife were out of work.

Narrowing the list, men in close proximity were out of the question. The young were eliminated due to inexperience, long painted nails and short skirts. Jess needed an experienced middle of the age group female with not only typing skills, but capable of running an office efficiently, including bookkeeping skills.

"Not an easy ask!" Gerald, in charge of recruitment, frowned, lighting his third cigarette. Adding as Jess began to rise from her seat, "Maybe I can get back to you tomorrow?"

Irritated by his indecision and lack of professionalism, Jess gave him her card and closed the door behind her.

Jess was feeling disgruntled as her paperwork was becoming unmanageable. Her phone was disconnected due to late payment, so she moved to the nearest phone box in the avenue and dialled Julia's number. "Hi, Julia, you couldn't loan me a secretary come bookkeeper for a few days? I'm sinking fast until I have everything up and running in the office."

"I've been expecting your call," Julia laughed light-heartedly. "I'll have someone sent over right away."

Feeling happy she could leave the paperwork to someone else, leaving her to do the things she did best, Jess returned to Robert, who was still ploughing through the antiques.

Lifting his head briefly, a look of intent concentration, Robert only half smiled. "I have never seen so many beautiful pieces in a loft before!" His comment stirred Jess's interest, not only financially, but a moment of nostalgia took her by surprise.

Stepping gingerly through the ones already labelled, Jess wanted to laugh. Covered in cobwebs and all manner of bird and other vermin droppings, Robert looked a sorry state. "Can I help?" She smiled as he shuffled uncomfortably under her glare.

Handing her a clipboard and gold pen, Robert's face changed from dismay to relief in seconds. "I was supposed to bring someone with me today, but Clifford has rang in sick." He took a deep breath, "Any help would be greatly appreciated." This time, his smile was more of a beam.

Reading a directory of listed objects from different eras, Jess began writing and labelling as Robert confirmed his findings. Lost in the moment, time passed quicker than first thought.

Jess left the loft to check on other issues. Not only the builders, who were making splendid progress due to the finances rolling in, but the gardeners and painters were gathered in the hallway awaiting her instructions.

Tasks seemed daunting, although confirmed by each craftsman that they were standard procedures, Jess hoped nothing would be left to chance.

After she stated her requirements, they left as the telephone rang, "Hi, is that Ms Turner?" the voice of Gerald from the agency, a little more awake, asked.

"Speaking," she answered, hoping he would get to the point without falling asleep.

"There's someone on the way you may find useful!" He stopped as Jess sighed.

Trying to sidestep him due to Julia's offer, "Err, sorry, there's someone at the door."

"That will be him!" Gerald answered quickly, closing the call.

Snatching the door open, she mumbled, "Fool, he knows a man is out of the question."

As she looked up, a tall, handsome, very smartly dressed young man grinned, "You haven't interviewed me yet!" He laughed a deep, manly laugh, "I can assure you I come with extremely good credentials."

Realising she was mumbling out loud, Jess, her colour rising, quickly added, "Yes… yes, please come in," embarrassed he had heard her ramblings.

Playing the injured male for effect, he said, "It's fine. Most people expect a female when requiring a secretary." His eyes were bluer and his teeth whiter than Jess felt comfortable with. "Christopher Collins, at your service," hand outstretched. "You can call me 'Chris'." He continued to smile.

Reading a Curriculum Viti to end all CV's, Jess felt ashamed. "Please excuse me. I'm not always this rude," she apologised.

"Well, should I leave now, or are you going to give me a trial?" He was still smiling a most disconcerting smile and Jess felt obliged.

"Of course," pointing to a typewriter unused for some time, Jess passed several overdue letters for reply.

Taking them, Chris sat confidently. Seeing Jess had already written notes as to her replies, he began.

Typing with speed despite the need to change the ribbon, the letter 'in tray' lessened and the out-tray was ready for signing.

There was no question this guy was good. Not only with his typing and grammar skills but also his working unsupervised was everything Jess could wish for. His only downside was that he was by far the most handsome of men.

Hoping to find a reason not to employ him, Jess asked, "Have you bookkeeping skills?" expecting the answer to be no, giving her a get out of jail card.

"I have many certificates in accounting. It's not really my thing, but as a package of duties, I'd be happy to oblige."

Reading the grades more befitting an accountant, Jess couldn't find a reason other than being honest about her preference for a woman, "I'm sure you will be fine," came out of her mouth before her brain could scream *no way*.

"Julia, I've found someone to help in the office. Sorry to mess you around, but this guy has qualities I couldn't refuse."

"You're kidding. A male?" Julia exclaimed, having been made privy to Jess's aversion to the close proximity of the opposite sex.

"He made it impossible for me to refuse," Jess replied, sounding more like an adolescent rather than a businesswoman of worth the words spilled out incoherently.

"He must have something special," Julia laughed, a note of curiosity in her voice.

Despite her reservations, Chris was the optimum of efficiency. The office was soon arranged to suit his tastes. It would have been difficult to find any woman to match his talents.

Professionalism personified, her words to Julia forced a laugh. "Don't tell me you have found the 'holy grail' of assistants?"

"He's very good," Jess added, not wishing Julia to assume that other than running the office, Chris was up for stud of the year.

Not leaving it there, Julia continued chiding. "And there, I thought you'd stopped looking?"

"Please… give me a break. Do you think I've learned nothing?" Jess thought of Mark and closed the call.

It didn't take long for Jess to see the benefits of not just Chris. With the suppliers and craftsmen now being paid handsomely, the transformation was astounding.

The many organisers and specialists Julia had suggested worked miracles. Although restored, every detail of the mansion looked natural and aged, just enough to convince everyone it had been maintained with care over the years.

Having agreed to sell some, but not all, family memories, a section containing many antiquities had been installed in the great hall exactly as Jess had instructed.

Coughing so as not to surprise her, Chris entered the gallery. "Morning, Jess, I have some papers for you to sign."

Turning toward the area hosting a selection of antiques, gesticulating with his hand, he moved around, taking in the carefully restored pieces. "Don't you think swags and tails would add to the ambience?"

Jess laughed, "Are you a connoisseur in the ancient order of tapestries as well as all your other talents?"

His face took on a more sombre look. "Sorry, I didn't mean it as a criticism. My father was a museum curator for many years and I spent time as a child learning from him."

"No need for sorry, Chris, I find it fascinating the extent of your knowledge!" Jess wondered why he had chosen to be a secretary and bookkeeper when his vast experience of so many things was evident.

Handing Jess a letter stamped urgent, Chris turned to leave. "Hand-delivered a few moments ago. I thought you would wish to read it right away!"

Feeling his discomfort, Jess took the envelope. "Thank you. I'll be with you soon to sign the post."

Tearing open the letter, Jess wondered if she had forgotten to pay a bill, as many had been put to one side before Chris arrived.

A letter from Julia's solicitors:

"Dear client,
Our attention has been drawn to an error in the perimeter to the left of your property. It would appear a section of land has been landscaped for which you have no title deed.
Please contact our office without delay.
Yours sincerely,
Abbott, Cousins, and Tatum solicitors."

Making her way through the garden, Jess assumed a mistake had been made even though the gardeners had used the latest plans to assess the extent of the plot well before planning permission had been granted.

Rebuilding part of the walled garden, which had deteriorated over the years, was undertaken, adhering strictly to the rules and measurements.

Calling the planners and gardeners to a meeting, it was agreed they would visit the planning officers to establish what had gone wrong.

Satisfied all would be sorted, Jess walked through the gardens with a smile on her face. The blossoms on the fruit trees were a joy to behold. Howard had done just as he had promised and the result was wonderful.

Deciding to walk the perimeter to the left of the garden, Jess was surprised to see work in progress on the land adjacent. "Hi," Jess called out, seeing a groundsman directing with his hand.

"Morning." The ruddy smile of an obvious foreman closed the distance between them.

Returning his smile, Jess stood on a rock, "Has this land been recently sold? I haven't seen anyone here before," she queried.

"I think so. It belonged to the Grenvilles. He recently died and left it to his daughters."

Wondering if she was discussing the situation with the wrong person, she waved and turned to step down.

"I think they said his name was Burnettie, a big wig in the city. Texas oil!"

Dread set in before she could answer, "Thank you, much obliged!" Jess sat on the rock feeling faint.

Mark may be many things, but surely not a stalker. A coincidence? A purchase made by his advisors without his input? Jess thought not.

The area surrounding her property was sought after for many reasons. The main one was easy access to amenities without the overcrowding of the city. Mark's property gurus would need just a nod to buy up land for him as an investment.

Trying hard to smother her disquiet, Jess made a phone call, having tried hard to decipher the signature at the bottom of the letter. "Good morning, may I speak to Mr Tatum, please? Jessica Turner speaking. I have received a letter concerning land adjacent to my property."

"Just one moment, Ms Turner, I will see if he's available." The voice of a very efficient receptionist echoed. *Must be a sizable building*, Jess thought to herself.

"Ms Turner, how may I help you?" Jess considered the question unusual considering the letter was signed by him only yesterday.

"It's in connection with a hand-delivered letter," she said, not elaborating, hoping he would recall his signing.

Taking a moment to search through his desk, "Arr, the land. It would seem encroachment is the issue." He hesitated, taking time to read what he had written.

"Mr Burnettie's agent raised the enquiry. It would seem an investigation is required. At the onset of their development, his architect discovered the oversight." He coughed before continuing. "A wall has been erected on his land."

"May I suggest Mr Burnettie or his advisors check the historic plans. The wall you refer to has been in place as part of a walled garden for centuries. My involvement has only been to have a section restored," Jess replied, sounding sharp.

"Hmm. I will convey your sentiments and write to you as soon as I have a response."

Before he could add more, Jess had closed the call. "Burnettie the powerful," Jess murmured to herself, "will find me an equal adversary should he take me to task!"

Chapter Six

Gavel in one hand, a hush action with the other, the auctioneer began. The room fell silent as the first exhibit was placed carefully on an easel.

This was a day Jess had been looking forward to. Not having joined the throngs of prospective buyers and seller before, it was a new experience long awaited.

Looking around the room for familiar faces, having mixed with the rich and famous during her time with Mark, Jess was surprised she recognised none.

This was to be a day of revelation, as many wonderful examples of the past had lain dormant for years, the auction house boasted.

The answer soon became clear with the arrival of a consortium of investors and museum curators, filling the rows just before the start.

"Been to the bar, no doubt," a stranger whispered as Jess settled, having moved along a line of neatly upholstered chairs.

Smiling her agreement, feeling uncomfortable as buyers of her sought-after treasures shuffled along rows reserved for the discerning, Jess hid behind her program not wanting to be recognised as the owner of such treasures.

Having checked her rights to the previous family's possessions, the sale of the dilapidated house having stood empty for many years, it was agreed and signed by the hierarchy of wills, codicils and heirs that no descendants could be found despite world-wide searching.

A rubber stamp was given in Jess's favour on the understanding she restored not only the buildings to meet regulations, but also the internal artifacts wherever possible. No mention of individual items on their appraisal, giving rise to the partial sale.

Julia's agreement to finance the restoration of the house for a half share in her future business, Jess was confident she alone was the artifacts genuine owner.

"The first item in your booklet…." A rustle of paper. "A portrait of the original owner on horseback with hounds…." Jess looked up. Tussled red hair, unmistakable amongst others, had Mark held up a flag. He couldn't have been more obvious.

Despite the humongous success of the auction, Jess couldn't wait to disappear. Hiding in the ladies' room until everyone left, the banker's draft attached to a list confirming individual sales blurred as she signed her acceptance.

"An enormous success," the auctioneer smiled, shaking her already shaking hand. The millions of dollars raised seemed insignificant compared to the chasm in her heart.

Why, after all this time and his callous rebuttal, did her heart still hanker for his touch? Jess asked herself.

The taxi arrived, she gave her bank's name, and Jess sat back in the seat feeling faint. Not with the size of the draft, but the realisation that all the money in the world couldn't compensate her heart's anguish.

"Julia, hi," Jess put on a brave face. "It was the sale of the century. Thank your restorers for me. Without their expertise, this unexpected gift wouldn't have been possible." A tear ran down her cheek.

"Why do I get the impression your delight is marred?" Julia asked as a sob from Jess couldn't be controlled.

"It's a long story. One I hope never to repeat," Jess left it there.

Julia felt uneasy, having heard the size of her good fortune. "Would you like me to come over?"

"I'm fine, really!" Her voice sounding vague, she replaced the receiver.

This was not the expected jubilation of Jess's fortune in the bank Julia had expected. Making for the garage door, "I'll have the car back asap," Julia spoke as her chauffeur, soap on a sponge, looked astonished.

Washing the screen and removing the remnants of his cleaning, Julia headed for the state highway.

Taking longer than expected, Julia jumped from her car and ran up the steps. Ringing the bell, heart in mouth, this was not the Jess she had grown fond of.

Jess was a shadow of the person usually so confident and smiling. It was a shock. "What is it, my friend?" she asked, taking her in her arms.

Between the sobs, Jess replied. "It's an old and long story."

"I have the time," Julia replied, escorting Jess to the sitting room.

The whole sorry tale out in the open, Julia was taken aback. "Life, as we know, can be complicated. Not many are excused the agony of heartbreak," she added, hoping her comforting words would help.

"An understatement." Jess, relieved to have shared her feelings, smiled a sad smile. "I am to blame. I let circumstances blur reality. I had no idea...." Hesitating, she wiped a tear.

Having experiences similar herself, Julia added, "You're not the first and you won't be the last. Love is not an exact science."

Jess offered the auction list to confirm her good news. "No need for a man's arm to lean on now!" Julia smiled, realising the fortune would enable Jess to live the life she had hankered for.

"Once that sentiment would have thrilled me," Jess stuttered. "Why does it not feel that way now?"

"Put on your glad rags. We're off for a night to remember," Julia said, making for the door. "Promise?"

"I promise!" Big sad eyes, hair awry, Jess tried hard to push Mark to the back of her mind.

The club was alive. Dancing, singing to a four-piece band, drinking Daniels over ice, the party started. Many admirers, some wealthy, some not so, flirted and cajoled the drunker the girls got.

How, Jess thought, *is this possible?* Back then, it was difficult to draw attention of even the gawkiest adolescent.

Catching a glimpse of herself in a floor to ceiling mirror, the answer was obvious. The stunning-looking woman that stared back, long red hair, tight-fitting burgundy gown, diamond jewellery most women would die for, she was the optimum of desirability.

Trying to fight back the thought of Mark, should she have found him after her financial transformation, who knows. Maybe, just maybe, they would be dancing together tonight.

The night to remember promised by Julia had been a resounding success. The offers of a lift home were stunted by, "I have my own chauffeur, but thanks anyway." Jess made her way home as Julia accepted a lift from a friend.

Girls together whenever the opportunity arose due to Julia's other business interests and Jess's restoration project, the pair lived life to the fullest.

Trips abroad to countries only read about before, the Caribbean was explored alongside the Far East and Europe, stopping off in Dubai, Singapore and London. The world was their oyster.

Soon to come down to earth as the project was nearing completion, grateful for the management of everyone involved, Jess inspected the results of their labours.

Everyone congratulated Jess for her foresight. All involved were richer, not only from dollars, but the experience gained was recognised as remarkable.

Standing back, admiring the opulence, Julia, Jess and her crew of multi-talented people, raised glasses of champagne.

Tears stained her immaculate features as the last of the people she had grown to admire waved their goodbyes.

Just a few were left to support her, Julia, Chris and Howard the gardener, now hosting a flotilla of trained helpers.

With lawyers, advisors and bank managers retreating to their respective offices, on call should she need them, Jess felt the loss of everyone's presence.

Looking forward to the recruitment drive headed by Chris for language tutors, deportment advisors, upper-class cultural tradition instructors, chefs, cleaners, the list endless, was underway.

"We only want the best," Jess advised as Julia nodded her agreement.

The school soon to be opened, preparations were underway with precision. "Everything must be perfect." The pair shook hands.

Showing parents and pupils around pleased Jess. She was familiar with all things required for their little darlings' future adult life.

It was as if by helping others, her own life changed. No swearing when things went wrong. Slouching was out of the question, as was an unsmiling face, despite her needs due to feelings of loneliness, even when surrounded by many.

She had a collection of dogs. Her favourite was Diesel the Staffy imported from England, alongside Jeremy the Afghan, whose gangly legs sprinted alongside, as their walks across manicured lawns were admired by the girls.

No surprise her nickname, 'pet lady', had stuck. She was proud to be in her dogs' company. They never questioned her judgment and loved her no matter what. *Unlike males of the species*, she thought, having encountered the unwelcome attention from yet another suitor offered up by Julia.

"Julia, please, no more prospective admirers," Jess laughed, having had an invitation from a man Julia considered an extremely good catch. "I have no need for male company. I'm happy as I am!"

Life, Jess decided, was perfect. Everything she wished for at her fingertips, her focus to help others took precedence over her once selfish horizon.

No more the struggles of the past, she grew with confidence that the rest of her life was secure come what may.

Jess's esteem grew with her bank balance. The local and wider world recognised her talent as a businesswoman and the charities that benefited from her generosity revered their benefactor.

Front page interest features often marvelled at Jess's ingenuity. Offers of fortunes to disclose her humble beginnings were turned down and she remained an enigma.

With her family still estranged, it seemed inappropriate to turn over stones better left alone. Jess felt sure her father would frown on her rise from pauper to princess, or was that from tart to queen?

Chapter Seven

"What?" Jess shouted hearing the news. "How can that be?" she questioned as the telephone rang.

"Yes, this is Jess Turner!"

The voice on the other end unrecognised, a bluster of words spilled out. "Is it true you were a hooker?"

Slamming down the receiver, Jess sat mortified. Chris, standing soldier-like murmured, "I have no idea what this is about!" He placed the newspaper front page in front of her. "It's nonsense," he added with a look of bewilderment.

Bowing her head, her shaking hand took the receiver, "Julia, have you seen the news?"

"No, but I've heard the radio. I give you my word I haven't murmured a word to anyone." A faulter before asking, "Are you ok?"

"Not really. I thought I'd put the past behind me." Obviously broken by the news, Jess asked Chris to bring in his notepad:

"Dear parents, you have no doubt heard the news. It is with regret that from tomorrow, the J & J foundation will be closed. Please arrange to collect your daughters as soon as possible.

I will arrange a refund for all ongoing lessons and thank you for your past support. Proprietor, Jessica Turner."

"Is that necessary?" Chris questioned, "Surely you will raise the question with the press?"

"I think not," was all Jess answered, walking wearily to collect her dogs.

Chris, completely baffled, answered the telephone best he could with, "Ms Turner's raised an immediate enquiry into the allegations." He closed each call hoping to quell the lies.

Taking the phone off the hook as he realised the hounds were baying, he spoke to Julia, "Can you come over? Jess needs you."

"I have my coat on. I will be there as soon as possible." Breathless due to her haste, Julia backed out the car.

She found reporters at her gate shouting, "Are you a hooker too?" and "You must have known. What have you to say for yourself?"

Wanting to raise two fingers, but thinking better of it, Julia drove on without uttering a word.

More reporters at Jess's gate, Julia pressed the horn. "Go away, you parasites!" she shouted, driving on hoping not to collide with the fools.

Chris opened the door with eyes out on sticks. "She's in the garden with the dogs. I've tried to speak to her, but she refuses to answer."

Julia a little more informed, tried to calm him down. "I will talk to her. Please don't worry. We will sort this thing out!" she added, handing him her coat as he opened the patio door.

"Jess!" Julia called out as the dogs turned, wagging their tails and jumping up to be petted. "Good boys," she said, seeing Jess sitting and crying.

"What am I to do? I have no idea who would do this to me." Hesitating, she thought of Mark. "I'm sure Mark would have said something before now if he intended to hurt me in this way." Sobbing, she held onto Julia.

"Mark wouldn't stoop so low. He may be unhappy you tricked him, but he will be as devastated as you."

"Only because he may be associated," Jess said dolefully.

"Think who else would want to hurt you? Maybe money is the object of the disclosure?"

Her mind a blank with the implications to her reputation, thriving business and charities she had grown to cherish, Jess was unable to recollect.

Taking her arm, Julia led her back to the house. "We will refute the allegations. Without proof, nothing will go to court."

"Word of mouth can be just as destructive to a business like mine," Jess added, holding her head in her hands.

Follow up stories came fast and furious. "A foundation or brothel?" The headlines shouted from front pages.

Disgruntled parents threatened to sue even though no proof was presented.

It seemed no one gave her the benefit of the doubt despite her previous reputation as a pillar of the community and defender of the sick and ailing through her charities.

Her cheques returned with return to sender clearly marked on the front, it felt like the end of the road.

That was until the phone call! "Remember me?" after several days of quiet after the storm, an unfamiliar voice spoke.

Gallant Chris, hands waving for Jess's Dictaphone machine to be placed by the mouth piece, quietly asked, "Who shall I say is calling?"

"Put the bitch on!" the male voice demanded, as Chris hesitated before replying, "Please hold."

It was obvious blackmail was intended as Chris summoned Jess slowly to the phone.

Holding the mouthpiece, he instructed, "Make your answers poignant."

"Jessica Turner here. How can I help you?" Jess tried her hardest not to scream 'bastard face me like a man'.

"You can best help yourself with a ransom of one million dollars. Chicken feed for someone like you!"

"When and where? Although there is no truth to your accusations, I will pay you to stop spreading malicious lies about me." Chris raised his thumb in agreement. The words had been recorded.

"A bag taken to the train station for safekeeping in the name of William Scofield. I will be watching you. Any police and I will make far more trouble than you can handle." The phone went dead.

"My God, William! He was the one that told Mark." Hesitating, not wishing to involve Chris in her past, Jess looked to Julia for support.

"I recall he tried to extort money from Mark!" Julia lied, hoping to sidestep Chris.

"Type out this message. I'll hand it to the police along with the recording. He'll find dealing with me more difficult than the police," Jess added to Chris, her old self coming to the fore.

Her dander was up big style, not only with William (Bill), but all the people who turned against her without giving her the benefit of the doubt.

"I can't believe the press who praised me for my good work, the parents without thinking me innocent until proven otherwise, even the charities sending back my cheques are baying for blood," she conveyed her despair to Julia. "Just when my faith in people had been restored after Mark, the people I had grown to respect and admire turned their backs on me." Jess felt devastated, but angry at the same time.

Speaking from the heart, Julia confirmed her support. "I've known the truth and didn't blame you for seeking a better life." Adding, looking Jess in the eye, "I've admired you from the start. You have qualities much sought after considering your beginnings. Only a fool would deride you without just cause."

Chris, forever faithful, even Howard dispersed the accusations as folly. It was a bitter pill to swallow but swallow it she would.

Her family was still estranged. "Get the press off my back or else," her dad's words stung, although her methods to reach her goal had been unorthodox. Not the word her dad had used, more, "You'll reap what you sow my girl, just you wait and see!"

His sentiments ringing in her ears, Jess realised how true his words had turned out to be.

Although accepting blame for her rags to riches plan, *Had I have realised the talents I possessed in the beginning, maybe things would have been different even with Mark*, Jess pondered, tears welling as she thought back.

"I'm sure he thinks I deserve everything I get," Jess whispered. Julia didn't answer, thinking it better until things settled down.

Still staunch in her regard for Jess, Julia quietly considered their options. Feeling sure they would succeed again no matter the turmoil of the past months, much had been learned since they first met and it would be a waste to throw it all away.

A new plan was needed. Jess was fond of plans and lists depicting her ambitions. "Nothing left to chance" was always the forefront of her thinking and next time would be no different, Julia was convinced.

Sticking close to her friend, seeing her change from victim to aggressor was a new experience for Julia. This would pass, she was sure, as with grief in bereavement, anger would subside, leaving hope from better memories in its wake.

Following the stamping and howling like a banshee, Jess became quiet and subdued. "They will see. I don't sit in the shadows licking my wounds," moving to another faze in the grieving process as the horror of her situation turned to revenge.

"The police will sort this out," Julia said quietly, wondering when the old Jess would return.

In one way, Julia was right. Following his arrest, William Schofield pleaded his innocence to anyone that would listen.

The turning point as the police produced irrefutable evidence of his guilt, he turned from pleading to swearing he would get even as he listened to his voice menacingly threaten Jess with all things unholy for a million dollars.

"It wasn't me," he began until another recording was produced of his original statement when his voice unmistakable, came back to haunt him.

All his screaming and protesting was quelled as William's arrest for aggravated blackmail was recited.

With hard evidence from voice experts, it was considered jealousy due to being turned down romantically had been his instigator.

The problem for Jess was her faith had been shattered in people that should have been on her side.

Back to square one was not an option. No more snooty parents with wayward girls needing to be tamed and forced to be something they blatantly refused to be.

No more charitable donations for stuck up parasites that took pleasure in her downfall after the begging bowl turned sour.

No more Mark, as his bitter last words had wounded her irreparably.

Jess was on a mission to discover new ways of using her good fortune without patronising the many that stood against her in her hour of need.

"I'll show them," her revised mantra. "If they want to believe the worst, then the worst is what they'll get," she whispered to herself, trying to decide how best to get even.

Chapter Eight

The house looked awesome as Jess walked her dogs. She stood back in wonderment. Nothing could change the improvements she had made to her life.

Counting her blessings, the main things left worth having were her home, her business partner, Julia, Chris, and Howard, now her close friends.

Jess's family was still aggrieved. She had hoped her dad would have a change of heart seeing the obvious benefits her efforts could afford him. If only she could reconcile the past and his aggression towards her.

Jess had loved the business she and Julia had built and would never forget the many talented people who had made her world and others' a wonderful place.

She admired the many bedrooms restored to perfection for debutants, the staircase, dining hall and ballrooms stunningly brought back to their former glory and used for educating ladies hoping for what she'd once hoped for: a comfortable life with a rich man on her arm.

Jess hesitated, *How come someone like me wishing exactly the same was ridiculed for trying to achieve it?*

Pondering the outcome, notwithstanding a male, on the one hand, quiet resignation, on the other, an overwhelming sense of belligerence, Jess lifted the phone.

"Hi Julia, I have a brilliant business idea!" She was smiling with mischief.

"Jess, great to hear from you. You sound bright," said Julia, a little reticent due to Jesse's previous malaise.

"I am. Can you come over? I have something I'd like to mull over with you," still grinning, Jess anxiously awaited her reply.

Julia, thinking a holiday in the sun or a cruise to top up a tan, agreed to meet up. "I'll be round as soon as. It's been ages since we talked," she answered, selecting a dress for the occasion.

What should have been a nice surprise turned out to be the opposite! "You want to do what?" The question hanging in the air like wet fish on market day.

Jess was grinning from ear to ear as she described her latest plan. "Together we can make it work. I have everything in place in my mansion. All we need is a recruitment drive, which as you know, Chris is a master of." Her excitement was overwhelming considering her previous, "all in good time!" when previously asked, what now?

"But an escort agency?" Julia was stunned.

"I have it all worked out. Only ladies of youth and good looks to begin with. Deportment, languages, and other finishing school advantages we can teach them as we go along. I will contact the team we employed before. Just think, Julia, it will be perfect."

Seeing the change as Jess danced around the room, Julia said, "But a brothel? What are you thinking?" She began speaking before Jess interrupted.

"No, no you have it wrong. Everything will be above board. A genuine business with genuine employees located in a superb environmental haven."

Stunned beyond words, Julia sat mesmerised as Jess gesticulated, "You want to use your mansion to entertain lustful men with only one thing in mind?" She couldn't believe her ears.

"Put crudely, yes, but my interpretation would be a high yield introductory meeting place for discerning males with money to burn." Jess clasped Julia's hands. "The girls escorted with the idea of a permanent relationship.

"No need to invest more. The venue is at our fingertips." Jess whirled around, indicating the potential.

Julia, sceptical, sat mesmerised as Jess rambled on. "Don't you see? Nothing would be wasted and the bottom line far more lucrative than before.

"The girls would pay for our teaching and an introduction fee each time we found a male participant. The males would pay for the privilege of escorting the girls with a hefty sum up front for the introduction. It's perfect. All we do is watch the money flow in."

Contemplating the need to bring back the old Jess and the potentially explosive repercussions, Julia deliberated the possibilities.

Jess's hand outstretched, a cat who got the cream expression, Julia found it hard to refuse. Although her better judgment whispered no, her hand shot out and the pair shook.

Her agreement to join Jess in her money-making venture, although in place without specifics, this was not as Julia intended.

A rest home for the elderly, a kennel, even a riding school, but this was something Julia had never thought of.

Adding quickly, seeing Julia's reticence, "You can be a sleeping partner if you wish?" Jess murmured seriously.

Hearing Jess's unintended gaffe, Julia said, "You expect me to sleep with them?" She began laughing.

"Now you've got it," Jess laughed as the penny dropped. "But only if you want to." She joked, hugging her friend, adding, "I knew something would entice you!"

Tears of laughter flowing, Julia relented, "Give me the details and I will check it out. But only on the understanding nothing untoward takes place!"

Lifting her fingers in a salute, "Honest." Jess, ecstatic that Julia hadn't thrown out her idea, blew an air kiss.

It took less than an hour to unveil her plan. Everything described had been carefully documented and Jess was in her element after days of deliberation.

The rules outlined before a licence to trade could be agreed had been researched carefully, not wanting to miss even the slightest detail.

Jess had studied every statute surrounding the process. Using her guile as well as her persuasive nature, her meetings with the regulators had been concise and stipulated under the heading of 'lonely hearts club'.

Agreeing in principle, the application awaited confirmation by the general assembly. This was the sticking point, as many members were renowned for their uncompromising stance on anything deemed untoward.

Jess wondered how sympathetic they would be to the idea of a 'man meets woman' venue on the outskirts of their town.

Looking under her glasses, the first member began. "We have dance halls for this purpose," she said, frowning her obvious disapproval.

"What about the young who don't dance? How do they meet?" questioned a more amiable male.

"It will surely turn into a free for all!" the third to offer an opinion added, shaking her head.

Jess was called to a further meeting which was worrying. "We are at a stalemate with your request. Would you spare a moment to confirm your intentions?" the chairman spoke courteously.

Standing, trying not to let her trembling hands show, Jess began, "It has been my experience," she looked around the room, "that many in our community, young and older, are finding it difficult to meet prospective partners for the right reasons. Not as it has been suggested by some."

Straight-faced, she nodded toward the chairman. "But to talk and discover one's compatibility with the other," a moment to reflect, Jess added as rehearsed, "Religion, family background, literary interest, work ethic, hobbies, etc.

"It is only then, when these issues have been established, are the participants invited to take further their involvement." A quick glance around. "Outside of our business," Jess insisted.

"During the process, tea and food will be offered, music in the background with nothing untoward allowed." Jess smiled toward the ladies, hoping for questions.

None were heard as the room was fixated by her professionalism. "I have gardens to stroll around in summer and many downstairs rooms inside (Jess emphasised 'downstairs') should our clients require privacy to talk. I welcome visits from your members!" Jess ended, smiling toward the chairman to encourage his agreement.

"God, that was a nightmare," Jess whispered, moving to Julia who had been waiting in the hallway.

Julia reached out, seeing Jess red in the face. "Well, what was the outcome?" Not knowing which would be her personal preference, yes or no, Julia smiled.

"They will write to me with the result of their deliberations." Jess was indignant she had previously been taken to task by strait-laced, well-placed individuals who had the power to dismiss her hard work. "Let's get a drink!"

The first drink went down without touching the sides. The second spluttered out as a familiar face entered from the rear of the restaurant.

"Don't look now, but Mark's just arrived!" Jess turned away as he made his way to his table.

"Would you like to go?" Julia asked as Jess shook her head.

Sizing up the situation, two men and two women, it was obvious Mark had moved on. "Why should I?" she questioned, "I have no need to hide. It's obvious he has forgotten me, so why leave?"

Although Julia could see her disquiet, they stayed for the meal. The waiter, recognising Jess, smiled, "Good evening, Ms Turner. What would you care to order today?"

As her name was spoken, Mark turned and his and Jess's eyes met as if a magnet fell between them. A gentle smile and a nod from Mark was all it took for Jess to remember the past.

Wanting to remove her eyes before her old feelings were revealed, a snatch of her breath, she turned back, wishing she had left before.

"Why do I still react this way? It's been years now and I'm still…" Tears welling, it was hard to take down the large glass of wine. "Why did he smile?"

"Whoa," Julia held her hand, the one with the disappearing wine. "So much for your resolve. Would you like to leave now?"

Afraid to stand, between the mix of gulped wine and a heart that pounded in her ears, Jess was unable to answer.

Feeling sad that her friend was still in love, Julia held her hand. "It's natural to harbour strong feelings. Time doesn't always heal wounds as we would like," Julia murmured as Jess sat staring at her food, afraid to look up.

"I know it's stupid, but I am jealous of the woman who is sitting at his side," Jess admitted, folding her napkin for the hundredth time.

Forcing down the food, the experience of speaking to the council chamber gone from her mind, Jess finally found her composure.

"The audacity of the man. How dare he smile. He accused me of betrayal and threw me out without explanation."

Julia looked up but said nothing.

It was a guilty secret that Julia was unable to explain. She wrote to Mark, disclosing how he had misread Jess's sorry tale and she feared it would endanger her and Jess's relationship.

The smile by Mark she knew was because of the letter. His promise never to divulge her well-intentioned disclosure made it hard for any future reconciliation.

Mark's anger was replaced by anguish, as unbeknown to Jess, he had shared her feelings wholeheartedly and now regretted his haste following Julia's letter.

The letter only added to his heartache. He had hoped buying land alongside her home would give him and Jess an opportunity to meet casually, reviving once more their relationship.

Sadly, he could see from her reaction in the restaurant that he was no nearer a reconciliation than he was when he attended the auction, spending far more millions than intended, hoping to give Jess a better life.

In his study, having arrived home from their night out, Mark regretted the presence of his sister.

No close association since Jess, his friend's well-meaning gesture backfired as the sound of her name compelled him to look back.

"There something about eyes," Marks first word in an hour. "They convey many things. If I wasn't mistaken, our shared stare spoke volumes. I'm convinced she still has feelings for me."

"Well, tell her! No use telling me!" His friend was unsympathetic, thinking any girl would be mad not to respond to Mark's advances.

"A promise is a promise. I made one to Julia. If I approach Jess now, how will I explain my change of heart?"

"Don't, just kiss her hard on the mouth and you'll be home and dry!" his friend smiled with a pat on the back.

"You don't know the girl I fell in love with!"

Chapter Nine

The agony of the unopened letter, a council emblem giving away the sender, Jess sat deliberating.

Her realisation that the answer to months of hard work sat before her, menacingly urging her to slit open the envelope, Jess was afraid to unveil the result.

A further rebuke of her good intentions following the furore surrounding her last was too much to bear.

"Well, what did they say?" Julia questioned, unable to pick up a reaction from her stare.

Taking a few moments before replying, "I haven't opened it!" stopped Julia in her tracks.

"Do you want me to come over?" Julia asked, realising this project had been more than just another business deal. "Give me ten minutes. I'm in town. I'll be there as soon as!"

Feeling foolish, her confidence shattered by the people she thought admired her, Jess feared another failure.

Julia's knocking brought her back from the memories she tried hard to hide. Jess opened the door. "It's over there," pointing to the hall table, she held her ears and squinted.

"It's ok, they agreed," Julia shouted, excitement breaking the barrier of Jess's hands as she flew into her arms. "The terms are exactly as you requested."

The pair jumped for joy with a mixture of tears and laughter. "I can't believe it. You should have seen some of the women. They looked like a hangman's jury."

Jess, reading the acceptance, felt overwhelmed. "We can make this work, I'm sure," she added, moving to the drinks cabinet.

"To success and all who succeed." They celebrated as "The J&J's Refined Escort Emporium" was born.

***

Life wasn't always fair to those who tried hardest, but Jess considered this to be a new beginning.

Her past put to one side, this time she was determined not to put a foot wrong. Despite her previous stance that "she would show them," Jess decided it would be her swan-song. "If this doesn't work, I will hang up my gloves," she whispered to herself.

A few adjustments and they were ready to advertise. Chris, now a staunch supporter of both Jess and Julia, wrote up an extravagant advertising campaign.

"I can see it now," he emphasised. "Join us for an evening of excitement and socialising. Free to all who wish to attend.

"I've arranged a full-page spread, not only in up market magazines, but also in the AARP, drawing

80

attention of not only the young, but an older audience," he romanced.

"I have pictures of many age groups enjoying themselves." Chris laid out full glossy photographs for Jess and Julia to choose from.

"We trust your judgment. Go ahead and place your favourites. I'm sure we will double stamp our approval." Jess was delighted to see his enthusiasm.

Howard, now in charge of many gardeners, waved his hand above his head as they approached.

Blossom arches and wisteria-covered seated areas were arranged at intervals for privacy. The lake was stunning with water lilies in full bloom surrounding a changing colour fountain.

"Welcome to my haven of love!" Howard satisfied he had captured the essence of their intentions, smiled a welcome.

"Who wouldn't fall in love in this wonderland you have created?" Jess beamed.

He felt satisfied he had achieved his objective. "See you later," he called out, feigning a bow as he offered them a rose.

Strolling the length of his perfectly mowed lawns, dogs wagging their tails happily, life seemed perfect.

Although Jess pushed love from her mind, her thoughts returned unwittingly to Mark. Having uttered many "if onlys" over the years, Jess was amazed by the clarity of the memory. His arms around her, his lips lingering as he murmured his undying love.

How could I have got it so wrong? she agonised as each step took her thoughts back.

The beaches where we made love under the stars, the warm sea as we bathed, holding each other until sunrise.

His hands seeking every part of me. Jess shuddered as she recalled his touch. Why now was it still so clear?

She was lost in bygone days when her every thought was of Mark. His hot breath on her neck, his mouth moving to her breasts. Her face reddened as she recalled each kiss on her body as he craved more.

Why now? she repeated, a moment of Déjà vu almost too hard to bear.

Finally succumbing to her memories, Jess sat on the grass as Julia ran with the dogs.

The aroma of his aftershave, his warm body as he lay on top awaiting my signal to fulfil their shared bond. A deep kiss, all it took for his emotions to turn to more, much more. A tear rolled down her cheek as her mind meandered.

The moment we reached ecstasy burned my every fibre, Jess recalled, almost bursting with the clarity.

How could I have lost such precious moments? Now sobbing, Jess tried hard to dispel the agony of losing the only man she had, or ever would love, from her memory.

"What's up, sweet pea?" Julia joked as the dogs licked Jess's face, removing all sign of tears.

"Taking in the splendour of it all," Jess answered, a double meaning as Mark drifted from her mind.

"I thought you were asleep sitting up," still jovial, Julia chided.

"Just daydreaming, that's all. Thinking how lucky we are!" she answered, seeing the joy on her friend's face.

Not expected with the euphoria of success, for hours Jess was unable to draw her thoughts from Mark. She smiled, celebrating on the outside, but secretly pining for the feel of Mark's arms around her.

Jess was unable, since his smile, to completely remove him from her thoughts. Each time she convinced herself she was still angry with him, the warmth of his mouth on hers returned again to haunt.

The night was set aside for employees, alive with everyone taking part. "Party time!" Chris shouted, taking hold of Jess's hand to dance. The music Julia had chosen was exciting and had everyone on their feet celebrating their good fortune.

As the rhythm changed, the signal to her brain struck once more. She was no longer dancing with Chris. Her undeniable ache for Mark was as strong as ever.

"Put him down," Julia laughed, as Jess clung to Chris, unaware she was holding him tighter than was appropriate.

"Sorry, Chris, the music and far too much wine clouded my judgment," Jess apologised.

Laughing, Chris replied, "I'm not. I was enjoying it!" he joked, seeing her embarrassment.

"He wouldn't take offence," Julia whispered. "He's gay," thinking no more heartaches for Jess should she harbour his desires.

Staff celebrations over, the opening day arranged to perfection, everyone was in their element.

The warm sun was a bonus. The lawn was laid out with tables laden with every delight, including wine from the cellar. Two bottles had been retained from the auction for themselves. The scene was set for a night to remember.

Cutglass goblets and silver tableware shone. Flowers from the garden adorned a spectacular treat for the two hundred and twenty invited to the opening.

"I had no idea you knew so many people," Jess smiled as Julia prepared to play the perfect hostess.

"You forget I'm from hierarchy. They're renowned for their enjoyment of any gathering which includes fine wine and food." Julia laughed.

"You mean these aren't customers?"

"Certainly not. They would spoil a good shindig," Julia laughed, continuing to change the place names to suit her knowledge of who was best to sit by whom.

Overhearing the conversation, Chris smiled. "Not strictly true. My advertisement in the top magazines drew many interested parties. It will be fascinating to see how many pair up," he smiled. "I will then charge for our services." His cheeky grin made Jess smile.

"Are you taking names?" she asked, seeing a pen behind his ear and clipboard in his hand.

"Never pays to miss a financial opportunity. Who knows, one meeting may lead to another.

"I have already suggested they consider a further visit. I will send an invite following an investigation into their background. That way, we will have them in the net without further advertising." Chris grinned, moving between the revellers.

Howard, dressed to kill in a suit chosen by Julia, struggled with his collar as he admired the fruits of his labour. "The flowers look good," he underestimated, smiling from ear to ear.

"Thanks to your exceptional skills," Jess replied, hardly recognising him in his new suit.

Chris, checking for name tags displaying J&J's emblem, he listed the people arriving. Anxious not to miss a trick, he carefully added their partner's name. Julia's invitees were excluded unless showing an interest. A clever ploy, handing them J&J's cards with a suggestion they join his tour of the mansion, Chris patted himself on the back.

The music varied to suit everyone's taste. Dancing and drinking champagne, "The food is to die for," one guest gushed.

Amplifiers placed at intervals around the garden echoed the sounds of the sixties as couples danced on the lawns, around the lake and between the fruit tree lined orchard decorated with fairy lights. It was a magical evening.

The night turned to morning with a rising red sky adding to the ambiance. "How could this not be a success?" Julia and Jess mused.

As dawn broke, not wanting to go home, some guests were invited to stay. Bedrooms were prepared for singles and marrieds. The intention, Julia explained, "Was to give everyone an insight into their business plan and what they had to offer futuristically."

The revellers drifted in and out of the breakfast room from early to almost lunch time, depending on their varying arrangements.

Chris had hastily called on kitchen staff to prepare a varied breakfast. Coffee was a must for the slightly hungover and 'hair of the dog' for those most in need.

"There is a long-drawn-out parade of potential clients," Chris clarified, having stayed up for all but a couple of hours before falling asleep on a chaise lounge in the great hall.

Handing out coats, slipping J&J cards in pockets, Chris made sure no one forgot the evening once the haze had lifted.

The party a roaring a success, he counted the potential clients, pleasantly surprised. "This is wonderful news. We have captured a very discerning clientele, no riff raff to dampen our reputation."

Julia laughed, "I can see we are going to have trouble with you. We need a varied audience, not only rich on rich, despite family preferences." She was thinking of Jess and Mark as a typical example.

Not looking up from his typewriter, Chris grinned, "I am aware. Just thinking of the many municipal inspections. We wouldn't like the doubters to get the upper hand before we start?"

"Touché," Julia smiled, realising there was nothing she could teach Chris about protocols.

Chapter Ten

Counting the cost against confirmed clientele, the three shook hands. Chris was the first to be congratulated. "Well done, you!" Jess said, jubilant with the outcome.

"What would we do without you?" Julia gave him a hug.

He was gratified his efforts hadn't gone unnoticed. "This is just the beginning," he smiled. "There is still much to be done to attract ongoing clients.

"I intend to have posters on billboards, in dance halls, bars, everywhere people meet hoping to find their perfect match." Taking a breath, "Not only that but in cinemas, indoor and drive-thru.

"In night clubs displayed in neon boxes depicting couples holding hands and many more venues yet to be explored." Chris took another breath as Jess and Julia sat mesmerised.

"Why not stand on the podium next to the President when he next addresses the nation?" Jess laughed.

With a look of determination, Chris added, "I'm negotiating something better!" grinning to tantalise. "A Times Square neon."

Julia and Jess stood open-mouthed. Silence as they pondered the cost, feeling a fortune would be needed, Jess was first to speak. "An adventurous enterprise, do you have costings?" she asked gingerly.

"I'm on it. All I need is for you to agree and I will begin right away," Chris replied with enthusiasm.

Julia, unable to remain quiet, deliberated. "Make no promises until we have checked the figures. Not only for the advertising outlay but staffing levels, food and drink if we intend to offer freebies." She paused.

Interrupting, Jess waded in, "Balanced against possible income!"

"Were you thinking of employing accountants?" Chris asked quietly, realising there was more to this than anticipated.

Julia laughed, seeing his disquiet, "Only if you add them to the costings!"

***

All things considered, Jess was satisfied with the outcome. Promotion for Chris to general manager, a recommended accountant named Jeremy Standish, a secretary, Harry Golding, and the office was staffed by what Julia considered to be the best money could buy.

Seeing the office laid out and running like clockwork, Jess questioned, "Where did these people come from?"

Julia touched the side of her nose, "It's not what you know but whom!" she joked, trying to avoid Jess's eyes.

Jess was unaware that Mark had influenced the decision. A phone call from Julia and two highly qualified people at a price their business could afford until subscriptions rolled in were made available immediately.

"A magic wand," was how Chris described it, seeing the transformation from clutter due to lack of time to inboxes emptied and outboxes bulging with perfectly worded and typed letters ready for posting.

The books balanced, quotations negotiated (also influenced by Mark), their bottom line was set to swell beyond her wildest dreams. "Julia, you're a genius," Jess romanced. "How do you do it?"

Thinking before she spoke, Julia said, "I have many who know of my reputation. I just pulled a few strings." Knowing the outcome should Jess discover her deception, Julia insisted Mark never divulge his input.

Sad but compliant, Mark promised, wishing things could be different. "Do you think there's a chance I could explain and apologise for my haste?" he asked many times of Julia.

Julia shook her head, unsure if now or ever would be a good time to explain his intervention. "Although you have acted with compassion, not sympathy, it would be difficult to explain in a way Jess would understand." Julia was thinking not only of Mark's but her own close relationship with Jess.

As the open day approached, the excitement and tension rose in equal measure. Finishing touches overseen by Chris, his entourage of helpers marching up and down straightening curtains, checking seating, fingertip testing for dust in white gloved hands, nothing was left to chance.

"Perfection's the name of the game," he instructed, feeling responsible should there be the minutest error. "What's happened to the candlesticks I specifically...." Before he could add the next word, Jess placed her hand on his shoulder.

"Stop panicking, everything is exactly as it should be. You and your team have done a splendid job. Now it's time to reap what you've sown."

Smiling, Chris took a deep breath. "I feel like I'm about to give birth," he grinned. "Whatever that feels like!" he finally laughed, realising he had been stressed for hours.

"I can't help you there. It's not on my agenda," Jess joked as the pair hugged.

Julia arrived dressed to kill. "You're not dressed yet? The guests will be here in less than an hour." Chris looked like a rabbit in headlights. "I can see I'll have to roll up my sleeves. You look ready to burst at the seams," she said, taking Jess by the hand, leading her toward the red carpeted staircase.

Howard and his gardeners arrived, followed by the kitchen staff dressed alike, all but the chef, who was suitably decked out in black and white checkered trousers and a traditional toque. Desmond, the butler, resplendent, awaited the first to arrive. The air was full of expectation as he pulled on his white gloves and reached for the silver plate in readiness for the invitations. Royalty couldn't have prepared better.

As Jess finally appeared at the top of the stairs, every eye turned. "Wow," Julia murmured. The transformation from overalls, wellies and hair in a bun at the back of her neck was remarkable.

Her turquoise silk gown with a corseted waist and trailing hem, a white bower trim showing just enough breast to remain modest, and her red hair sitting high in curls on her head framing a film star face took everyone's breath away.

Julia flew to her side. "You look stunning," she whispered as Jess's face lit up.

"Likewise," Jess replied, checking herself in a mirror, her mind wandering back to Mark. *You should see me now!*

"Stand by your beds!" Desmond shouted, opening the entrance doors as the first limousine pulled up.

Agency valets stood in line, opening car doors as guests alighted. More designer wear in one place than Jess had seen in a lifetime, even Julia was impressed.

Taking ladies' wraps and gentlemen's coats, a host of bellboys ferried their outer garments to a cloakroom under the grand staircase. Desmond, looking regal, announced couples two at a time as Chris made notes should anyone arrive alone.

Ushering the carefully selected, suitably regaled young women and handsomely dressed young men to the great hall, the real purpose of the expense began.

The heady scent of floral arrangements coupled with a variety of the most expensive perfumes, almost exceeded Howard's flora and fauna. Beaming as the guests spilled out into his garden, hearing their glowing observations made all his hard work worthwhile. Smiling, looking every bit a gentleman, he approached Jess.

"Suitably impressed?" his arm held out for escorting her to the magnificent marquee. Laid out enroute to the lake, snacks and champagne in garlanded enclaves, every detail to impress had been considered.

"It's wonderful," Jess said, proud to hold Howard's arm. His efforts reflected on the lake in the moonlight. "What would we do without you?"

"You don't have to. This pleases me more than words can say!" his smile turning to a grin as Jess kissed his cheek.

The entrance to the mansion was festooned with fairy lights he had instructed to be placed around the doorway. "No doubt your invention?" she smiled as the limousines approached.

His reply was unheard as a familiar cream pearlized vision from the past rolled up. Concerned, Howard stopped. "Is everything ok?" he asked, worried he had somehow made a mistake.

"No, no, it's everything we could have hoped for and more," Jess turned, stumbling over her words. "…Thank you, Howard, it's beautiful," she reassured, squeezing his hand.

93

"Thank you, ma'am," his exaggerated grin signalled his content.

"See you later." She was still shaking as the uncanny resemblance struck hard.

Seeing Julia welcome a woman she thought she recognised from the restaurant, Jess was sure her escort was Mark.

Shocked, she sat in an alcove of wisteria covered for privacy, staring as the guy kissed Julia on the cheek. "I must have it wrong," she thought aloud, rising to continue her stroll to the house.

If Jess was shocked, it was more like a spear through the heart for Julia, as she realised the occupants of the limousine were Mark and his sister.

She wanted to ask what the hell he was doing here until a kiss on the cheek and an invitation clearly stating Mr Mark Burnettie and his partner stared her in the face. "Mark, pleased to see you and Angela. What a wonderful surprise."

"The bloody understatement of the century," she whispered as their names were read out for all to hear.

What to say to Jess, who she spotted making her way along the path leading towards her, she had no idea!

How to explain his arrival, let alone the kiss on the cheek? Julia ran to meet her. "It's not what you think!" were Julia's first words, out of breath, not from the run but from the sheer agony of the situation.

"What don't I think...?" Jess questioned as her worst nightmare dawned. It had been Mark, after all!

Chapter Eleven

Smelling salts shook Jess awake. Julia was grateful her fall had been onto the lawn and more grateful Chris was at hand to help.

Carrying her gently to the summer house, the pair tried to reconcile their thoughts. "What happened back there?" Chris innocently enquired.

Unable to explain, Julia shook her head. Although she'd welcomed Mark, it escaped her as to why he was here. The last thing she wanted was to upset Jess when everything had begun so well.

They struggled to open the door and lay her down without hurting her further or damaging her flowing gown.

Thinking aloud, Julia mumbled, "Why here? Why now?" The answer escaped her. It would be impossible to explain to Jess the kiss on her cheek.

Although her association with Mark and his sister was well documented, their arrival would be the death nell for Jess.

It was unlike Julia to panic, but there was a stirring in her chest as Jess sat stark upright and spoke, "You mean you had no idea?" rendered her speechless.

Not having a clue what was going on, Chris, bewildered, whispered, "Idea about what?"

Speaking across Chris, Jess looked deep into Julia's eyes. "Was it you?" tears seeping down her beautifully made-up face.

Julia's answer was blurted out, almost incoherent. "No Jess, I was as shocked as you!" her words trembling, she tried to explain.

Jess took a moment to inwardly digest her answer. "If it wasn't you, who else would be so insensitive to invite my ex?" She looked toward Chris.

He was scared he had made an unforgivable gaff. "Please, Jess, what did I do?" he frantically asked, seeing her holding her head in her hands.

Not wishing to hurt his feelings more, Jess whispered, "It was you Chris, wasn't it?" as Julia hugged her.

Chris's face changed colour. "What was me?" he asked, still in the dark as to their conversation. "Whatever it is I've done, I'm so sorry!" he added, holding Jess's hand for reassurance.

Still in shock, Jess answered kindly, "It's ok," (although it wasn't). "You invited my ex. It's a long story," she added, patting his hand in recognition of her understanding. "I'll be fine now. You get back to the guests." She spoke softly as he looked bewildered.

Julia, realising Chris's unfortunate blunder, said, "He took great care not to miss anyone from the guest list and with Mark a prominent presence in the town…." Julia hesitated, feeling heartbroken this would mar Jess's enjoyment.

Jess rose and brushed grass from her gown. "Let's face the fray." She lifted herself up and headed towards her private quarters.

Seeing Jess's determination had replaced the shock, "I'll help with damage!" Julia tried to smile.

The pair silently checked her gown for grass stains, wiped off old makeup and added new. "You still look amazing," Julia finally spoke as Jess grimaced.

"On the outside maybe, but not on the in..." Not finishing the sentence, Jess smiled a pretend smile in the mirror. "Onwards and upwards!" her old self, rising to the fore as they made their way to the staircase.

Jess was shattered to see Mark dancing with his lady friend, the one she had seen him with at the restaurant. "This is harder than I thought," she turned to Julia for support.

Julia realised the game was up. "It's his sister," Julia confessed.

"You know her then?" Jess questioned, a note of cynicism. Giving Julia no time to reply, she turned to leave.

Reaching gently for Jess's arm, lifting her hand for two glasses of champagne, Julia cautiously led her down the stairs.

Breathing deeply to lessen the impact of a face to face with Mark and with no intention of letting Julia off the hook, Jess lifted her glass, "To Mark and his sister!" Hesitating for a second, she grinned, "William's not on the guest list as well by any chance?"

Feeling the tension ease Julia smiled, a first for an age, "I think not. Chris is familiar with that slime ball."

The ice broken, the girls linked arms in a show of solidarity and entered the dance hall with a smile.

Meeting and greeting, the hands shook were innumerable. Mingling, Jess collected a glass of wine and moved to the left as Julia, a plate full of goodies, turned to the right.

Taking a moment to savour in the splendour, Jess stopped to chat with the judge who had granted their licence. "Good evening, Judge, I trust you're enjoying the evening?"

"It's splendid. What a transformation to the manor house. If only old Silas were here to see it."

"You knew him then, Judge?" Jess questioned as they studied his picture hanging on the staircase wall.

"Vaguely, when I was a lad. He was quite a character. Not one to cross, as I recall." Laughing, the pair went their separate ways.

Jess stepped back for a tray of champagne to be balanced through the revellers. Back-to-back, nudging as she made way, his breath on her neck and the smell of his aftershave was unmistakable. Jess froze as old memories flooded back. Even now after so long, it seemed like only yesterday. As he spoke, Jess thought she was dreaming. The "Hello, Jess" sent shivers down her spine.

His hand on her shoulder rendered her unable to move. How to respond. The old Jess would have had a quick retort, but the new Jess awaited his next words.

"Remember me?" he murmured as he moved to face her.

With a monumental effort, Jess returned his smile, the brightest she could muster. "How could I forget?"

She stood, looking like the answer to his prayers. "How indeed!" his breath taken with the image he was unable to forget.

"What brings you to my humble abode?" Jess replied, still smiling a forced smile. The sound of her heart rushing through her ears made his answer difficult to hear.

"Humble?" he hummed. "It's beautiful!" He whispered, not moving his eyes from hers. "Would you care to dance?"

Moving from static to automation, Jess held out her arms in a waltzing fashion. No reply, her body language was unreadable. Mark took her in his arms. The heat rising between them was unmistakable. Jess held her breath, afraid a sigh would escape, explaining more than words the height of her emotion.

She tried hard to concentrate on the music. *Why now?* It would be easier if he was still angry. *What's changed?* she asked herself as she danced on autopilot.

Not as sure of herself as the old Jess, the dance floor drifted from beneath her feet as he held her close.

His body language said everything as his spontaneous response was obvious.

The longer they danced, the more his physical reaction spoke louder than words. Following the nightmares of the past, all reservations disappeared as they looked into each other's eyes. He guided her to the garden.

"I still love you desperately," Mark's warm mouth seeking hers, he confessed. Jess, despite her previous reservations, was unable to resist and what happened next was beyond reasoning.

The summer house was locked from the inside, blinds drawn, still no words as he removed her elegant gown, revealing all through her see-through underwear. His intake of breath said it all.

Well, not all, as his own undress revealed his desire. Only heavy sighs and whispered undying love broke the silence.

The murmured, "I'm so sorry for the past," from Mark was answered with her finger to his lips, followed by an intense kiss marking the end of her anger and his restraint. Their passion exploded.

Time seemed of no consequence as they lay in each other's arms. The music and laughter of other revellers paled into insignificance compared to the intensity of their reunion.

With promises that the past would remain unspoken, it seemed their chance encounter had changed their lives forever. *Thank you, God!* passed though Jess's mind as they drifted effortlessly into the next encounter.

Who could have imagined this night arranged for the celebration of her success would end with another more precious as Mark, oblivious to the evening ending, kissed her gently as they celebrated once more their reunion.

Julia's voice could be heard above the guests' frivolities. "Where are you, Jess? The guests are starting to leave. We need you!" broke the spell.

She hastily replaced her gown, zipped up by Mark as he planted a hot kiss on her shoulder. "Here I am, just taking a break. Sorry, did I miss something?" Jess shouted her reply as Mark lay on the floor displaying exactly what she would be missing.

As Jess appeared from the summer house to greet her friend. "I'm not surprised you've been resting. You looked shattered," Julia smiled. "The evening's almost over and we must thank the guests for coming," she added, leading Jess by the hand.

Not having seen Julia all evening, Jess said, "Yes, it's been quite a night." She smiled thinking, *and how!*

Seeing Mark later fully dressed, looking handsome and suitably satisfied, her heart skipped a beat. He smiled, not giving away their secret as time would soon reveal his intentions.

"Thank you for coming!" her double-edged meaning not going unnoticed, Jess stared directly into his eyes as she held out her hand.

Not shaking, but kissing the back of her hand, he lifted his eyes, "It's been a pleasure!" Mark's reciprocating inuendo said it all.

The moment for Jess's revelation drew nearer as the last of the guests' limousines disappeared. The musical instruments loaded, the outside bar dismantled, the splendid marquee would have to wait until tomorrow. The clean-up began.

With many hands to the ready, the last of the entertainers said their goodbyes, looking slightly less elegant in their jeans. Jess busied herself, hoping to keep her secret a while longer.

Making for the stables the next morning, she took Julia's hand. "Let's ride?" Jess whispered as the stable boy collected the dogs. "It's more private through the woods. I think I owe you an explanation."

"Me too!" Julia surprised her with her retort, sitting astride her favourite mare.

"You first, I have a feeling it's going to be a long ride," Jess smiled, cantering faster until they reached the clearing.

The trees were alive with birds as the afternoon sun beamed through the leaves. The clearing held a special place in Jess's heart. She had spent many hours here thinking of Mark and wondering how it had gone so wrong.

Her dogs chasing rabbits, the horses grazing, the pair knew it was time to reveal their secrets.

Julia was first to speak, "I'm afraid I broke our promise!" her heart beating faster, thinking she may lose her friend's trust. "I wrote to Mark explaining your past and how hard you had worked to build a new life." She stood facing Jess, tears in her eyes.

Jess held out her arms. "I'm not angry, I'm grateful. I know why you did it, his actions explained." Jess hugged her friend as more dialogue was unnecessary.

It took only a moment for Jess to elaborate and relate the events of the evening, "I tried to resist, but the thoughts and feelings of the past overwhelmed me. It was as if we hadn't parted."

The ride back was for celebration, not retribution, as Julia had first thought. Nothing, it would seem, could separate the pair. Wind in their hair, sun on their faces, happy at last the past was behind them, a new horizon seemed nearer.

The view of the mansion as they approached was spectacular. No doubt their business venture would succeed. Why wouldn't it with two like-minded, hard-working women at the helm. Jess's transformation from rags to riches now written in stone, the world was their oyster.

Chapter Twelve

The words ringing in his ears, "Happy now?" from his sister, Mark held her high and swung her around. Ecstatic would have been a better way of describing his emotions. At last, he had everything. No more searching for someone to warm his bed. His love was returned and life was as good as it gets.

Working seemed easy, playing even easier as they celebrated their reunion. Real love had always been the missing link in Mark's wealthy, privileged life. Many had said he had it all, but that was never the case until now.

They went on holiday off the coast of Tampa Bay to seal their reunion. Despite phone calls Jess made to and received from home, she spent hours in Mark's arms.

Strolling along beaches, sunbathing in secluded coves, swimming, water-skiing and making love under the stars were memories neither would forget.

Mark was extremely generous, as Jess recalled from before. Nothing was too good for her despite protestations she had fortune of her own. "Gifts from the heart are the greatest of all," he whispered, placing a diamond bracelet around her wrist.

Idyllic was how she portrayed her holiday to Julia, having been given the good news their agency was progressing better than expected.

"I can't wait to see you!" Chris was surprised by her admission. Had it been him, he would have stayed forever in Tampa's paradise given half a chance.

"Of course, I'm having a great time, but that doesn't mean I won't be pleased to get back at the helm," Jess smiled to herself, having listened as Chris explained how many new clients he had secured from his latest advertising campaign. "I'll be back soon!" she replied to his surprise.

The closing remark was overheard by Mark as Jess put down the phone. "What now? Can't those idiots you employ handle the workload?" Mark sounding sharp, questioned.

"Of course, but our business was just beginning when I left," Jess murmured, thinking he would understand.

"I have managers to handle my business," he replied, slightly less aggressive.

Feeling uneasy with his quick retort, Jess smiled, stroking his hair with affection, "Let's not spoil what time we have left." Offering her hand, she indicated the bedroom.

"Sorry, I didn't mean to be critical. I know only too well the rigours of business," he drawled in his sexy Texan accent.

Leaving the hotel to join Mark's cruiser for the journey from Tampa to Miami, Jess stopped in her tracks. The message at reception from Julia to contact her urgently saw Jess wave to Mark as he sat impatiently in the limousine.

His latest harsh, "What now?" was a red rag to a bull as Jess mimed a telephone action.

"Julia, it's me. Do we have a problem?"

The line was sketchy and Jess had difficulty hearing, "They've done what?" the question hanging in the air as she tried hard to understand.

"….suspended our licence."

Jess failed to take it in. "Our licence," she repeated. "Why?" She pressed the handset closer to her ear.

She tried to relay the setback, as it was just as hard for Julia to digest the answer, "They've had complaints!" Her words were slipping in and out of range as they spoke.

Jess, trying hard to hear and grasp the implications, raised her voice, "Complaints from whom?" The line went dead before Julia could reply.

The only solution in Jess's mind was to return as quickly as possible. "Mark, I must go home. There's a problem. Can you drop me at the airport?" Grateful her luggage was packed for their onward journey, Jess was shocked by Mark's reply.

"No way! This is our holiday." Turning to the chauffeur, he instructed, "To the port and make it quick."

Before more could be said, Jess banged the boot, "Open up, I want my luggage." Angry that Mark took her business so lightly, her instincts for doing the right thing by Julia returned with a vengeance.

The chauffeur looked toward Mark to confirm her instruction. "If you don't open this boot immediately, I will leave without my luggage." Hand out, Jess hailed a hotel taxi.

The boot shot up and Jess didn't look back. Mark looked on amazed. "Please?" his hands upturned in shock as Jess's taxi drove away.

She watched as the taxi joined the traffic. "To the airport and be quick," Jess was more determined than ever.

Mark, resigned he would never tame his lover if he lived to be a hundred, relented. "To the airport and hurry." He felt sure when he explained, Jess would see sense and continue their holiday.

The plane took off, Mark upfront with the upper echelon, Jess upstairs in the lounge. Glass in hand, she reflected. *What's so hard to understand? My business is important to me, not forgetting the welfare of the people I employ.* Trying to control the imminent tears, she drank more wine than expected.

Climbing the stairs, resigned once more to being the peacemaker, Mark sat down. "Jess, what's the problem with you? I have lawyers dealing with real emergencies day in day out."

Jess, startled he had followed her, scowled instinctively with his 'real emergencies' comment. "Don't you get it? This is just as important to me as your business is to you. And no, I don't have lawyers coming out of my ears, but that doesn't mean……" His kiss halted her protests.

"Jess, this is new to me," he replied, holding her hand. "I have no idea how to handle your transformation." Making eye contact he added, "I love you!"

"Mark," she softly whispered. "There's no need to handle me, just love and understand I have a different life now. One I wouldn't change for anything, or…" she hesitated, "anyone!"

Not understanding, but going along with her protestation, thinking she would come around given time, Mark hugged his acceptance.

Leaving the plane, not knowing what hit her, the press and spectators awaited her arrival. Expecting the old cliché 'You a hooker?' remembering back, Jess was surprised to hear the word 'brothel'.

Jess ran forward as Julia and Chris greeted her. "What's this all about?" With no chance to talk, as shouting and forcefully directed microphones pushed forward, the three ran to an awaiting taxi.

Mark held back, making for the phone bank. "I need your help!" The words spoken softly to his lawyers, he stayed at the airport awaiting his limousine.

"These are outrageous accusations and my client, Jessica Turner, will forcefully deny all the claims." Seeing the might of the esteemed lawyer Francis

Woodward outside the gates of her mansion, the press withdrew without further comment.

"Thank you for coming so quickly, Francis. It was getting out of hand here." Mark turned to Jess. "Explain to Francis." Flustered, realising Jess was right to be concerned, he held her hand.

"I don't have all the facts, just what Julia explained and the newspaper reports," Jess, almost in tears, explained. "Give me time to discover the details and I will be better placed to handle whatever it is!"

"With respect," Francis, forever the professional, confirmed, "you have no need to do more. Leave the details with me and my team. I'm sure we will discover their error." Seeing the crowd disperse, they went their separate ways,

"Do you need me?" Mark's phone conversation from his apartment slanted as Jess was in tears. "I'm confident Francis will sort it out. He's the best there is." He was unable to receive an audible response as Jess stayed silent. "He will be in touch as soon as he has all the facts," Mark continued, slightly less sympathetic.

Bells ringing with his immediate response to her problems, Jess sat mortified. Hoping her thoughts as to what to expect in the future, Mark's controlling ways from the past struck hard.

Realising he had a lot to learn of her new intransigent stance, not only regarding her business but also her mindset, their rekindled relationship was set to be an uphill struggle. Jess sat wondering if he would ever see her as she was now or if he would crave the girl he fell in love with.

With more questions than answers, her business and her relationship were on the brink. The more she rationalised, the more complicated it seemed.

It's not as if she hadn't been here before. She had, but this time was different. A more grown-up and stronger Jess had pushed her way through the pupa of life, wishing to be a butterfly free from the constraints of the past.

No reversal was possible. No more a slave to convention, the way ahead was inevitable with or, she sadly thought, without Mark.

He had been right about one thing. Francis had done a sterling job. More facts and figures than any government could have established, the court case crumbled with compensation granted for the damage to her business substantial.

Handshaking all round, the final nail in the coffin of her critics, it was business as usual.

"We must take care in future who we welcome into our agency. Either that or a drastic change to our process is needed," Jess smiled, thinking maybe her original idea of being a madam housing more than willing and good-looking participants for the pleasure of eager rich males may be the way forward.

Julia frowned, "It's true you can't be tried for housing a brothel twice," she smirked, thinking Jess was joking, until she turned seeing the grin on her face. "You're not serious?" was met with another grin to challenge any cat with the cream.

Chapter Thirteen

The demographics of their different lifestyles were a stumbling block in the way of a happy ever after. He was an empire builder who considered her business venture tacky. Jess hoped for a closer relationship, not a marriage exactly, but certainly not spending her days as his mistress.

She was disappointed when he considered her not to have changed, wanting nothing more for her than enjoying shopping, the gym, having her hair styled, nails painted and generally being spoilt.

This was far from the newly independent Jess. She had hoped he would be prepared to help, rather than hinder, her efforts to build her and Julia's business.

Although Jess, aware of the previous pitfalls of their relationship and how she now valued the independence her new life offered, Mark, having made the first move to resort to what they had, was stunned to realise her determination to succeed had taken on a life of its 'own' and her need to be self-sufficient, alongside her developing business acumen, seemed a threat to his manhood.

Being from a family of the 'men work and the women weep', he was devastated to discover she had no intention of returning to their previous arrangement.

The only part she would concede was their lovemaking. Always having been an extraordinary passionate and considerate lover, Mark was confronted with a challenge he considered almost insurmountable.

Jess's refusal to give up her life to make herself ready for his return home without concession, made Mark question his decision.

Although the love they shared physically was better than ever, the failure to reconcile their differences drained their resolve. Far from what he had hoped, Jess became more determined to build a life of her own and a business the envy of her so-called betters.

Frustrated when she was not home to welcome him with a glass of his finest whisky and a welcoming bed to make love in, he found their role-reversal intolerable.

Jess would ring, apologetic something needed her attention and she would be delayed, pleading he drive over later to make love. His insistence this would have to end and a more conventional relationship be established made Jess baulk.

Having no intention of stepping back into a world she once coveted, saw both she and Mark at opposite ends of an eternal triangle of accusations and anger. "If we were married," Mark had shouted, "I would divorce you!"

"No need. It won't cost you a penny as things are," Jess's angry retort stung even harder.

Nothing he said or did could convince her to cave in. No threat to take back the car she treasured, a gift for her birthday. A smart rendering of, "I can afford my own," as the keys were flung across the room with a look of defiance, was the last straw.

"Why, when I love you so much?" Mark questioned in a moment of utter despair.

In a calmer voice, Jess replied, "You still think of me as a mistress with no life of my own. Sorry, Mark, I have changed."

From bad to worse, you would think, as they vied for a position of superiority. Jess, with her eagerness to detract Mark from her new resolution to change the purpose of her and Julia's business. Mark, still commuting between Texas and New York in an effort to appease her, hoping the tide would turn in his favour and she would come to heel, as did his mom in his dad's day.

"No chance!" Jess conveyed to Julia, as their agreement they dipped their fingers in a world far from their original plan was underway. "I have no reason to be his mistress. His original rejection taught me many things, mostly that I am stronger and more determined not to be what others need but to be myself at all costs."

***

So, the next phase in the life of J & J evolved. Men escorted in on the pretext of wishing to find a lifelong partner. Girls at the ready with a tempting array of provocative attire, the sky was the limit as the revenue achieved was received with little or no effort.

No one could criticize the deception that had been put to bed at the trial so aptly conducted by Francis Woodward. Nothing could be gained by complaining, as the case against a brothel had been well and truly put to bed by the best of the best.

Jess was adamant that the rules be adhered to without exception. Julia had hoped to turn a blind eye but was surprised she also enjoyed the questionable practices. "It's a far cry from my hoped rise to fame!" she confessed, banking the revenue offshore.

Jess laughed, seeing more than one of her accusers arrive incognito. "Good evening, Jess, nice evening for it!" was heard more than once, boosting her morale as well as her bank balance.

The liberation of the sixties greatly helped to realise their goal. Music was provocative like never before. No drugs were allowed, but alcohol sold at inflated prices was encouraged without fear of reprisal.

Night turned to day as their business flourished. The only downside, the washing machines worked constantly, assuring their clients' cleanliness was next to Godliness, which couldn't be said of their other activities.

"Do you think God will forgive us?" questioned Jess as Julia laughed.

"He frowned on Sodom and Gomorrah and Sarah turned to salt, so the story goes. So maybe we will have only one foot in St. Peter's gateway!" Still laughing, Julia ordered the latest in lace see-through underwear.

Off duty, their girls were happy. Paid well and with a more upper-class clientele than expected, what wasn't there to like. Satisfaction was the name of the game, not only for the gents that prevailed of their hospitality, but the ladies of the night who grew to enjoy the dollars and J & J's working environment in the bedrooms, as well as the downstairs splendour Jess's mansion had to offer.

Agreeing to Mark's requests, she joined him for at least one week every month on his ranch and when in New York, they spent time in his penthouse. Not only did she not want Mark to visit their newly reorganised establishment, but the idea she was out of his control for most of the time suited her ongoing ambition.

If he did wish to visit, Julia and Jess arranged a time when the mansion was closed for supposed decorating or some other concocted reason. Riding parties arranged with food and wine served by the lake, the less Mark saw of the mansion, the better. He rarely reached the staircase leading to the bedrooms before Jess suggested they make love as before in the summer house.

"So romantic! I'll never forget our reunion," was her one excuse, or a more modern approach, "Let's make love under the stars. I know a perfect place?"

The time spent on his ranch was a different matter. Mark's idea of a perfect day out was a rodeo, a pig roast, or riding the range checking the cows, not forgetting his latest oil well. Far less romantic than her ideas, but nevertheless, their lovemaking at the end of the day progressed from passion to another level learned from her more recent encounter, listening to their newly appointed sex therapists back home.

Massage parlours, saunas made for two and a private swimming pool were available at an extra cost. Individual dining areas with a wine list of specially imported champagne, also at an extra charge, the facilities were endless. The more their reputation grew in male circles, the more the dollars flowed in.

Outward respectability was essential to keep the critics at bay and Chris, now managing director, was as effective as always. Claiming he had a nose for sham clients had seen his rise through the ranks with Howard overseeing clients' shenanigans in the summerhouse and gardens, taking the accolade as head of landscape gardener with a pay grade to match his talents.

Jess and her partner in crime lived the 'life of Riley' on her weeks away from Mark, explained away as overwork. Julia and Jess flew to the most exotic places. The Seychelles, Maldives, Maui, Bali, the list and costs were endless.

Feeling free to do as she pleased saw Jess move further away from Mark, but not so much so that he became suspicious, "Darling, you work too hard. Would you fancy a break riding the range with me?" he asked to Jess's horror.

"Yes, that would be fun!" her reply was far from the truth, as a sore backside and dust in her eyes would be as far from a happy occasion as would a walk in a snake pit in the dead of night.

Mark was excited with expectation. "We can take tents for nights under the stars. As I recall, under the stars is your favourite position!" he grinned at the prospect.

"Tents, why not?" Jess could think of a million reasons, but none more so than after a day sweltering under a Texan sky.

The flight was set for the following week with an agreed stay of just two weeks, "Julia, I can't think of anything worse. What's more, I have nothing to wear!"

"Would sack cloth and ashes fit the bill?" Julia laughed at the thought of two whole weeks in blistering sun and making love with the possibility of being disturbed by a 'black-tailed rattlesnake' in mid-flow of passion.

"Very funny. If you don't stop now, I will suggest you accompany me!" Jess grinned, trying on a Stetson for size.

"Wild horses couldn't drag me along," Julia added insult to injury with her quip.

As much padding as the store could oblige was Jess's suggestion as they shopped for her trip. "Do I look big in these?" she laughed, seeing the size of two in her leather pants.

Still not convinced her friend would stay the course, Julia offered to take her to the airport and wait with her until the flight took off before returning to her own comfy bed. "Making sure I don't renege at the last minute?" Jess asked, wishing she had forgotten her passport.

"You'll be fine. You know he'd do anything for you. Suggest a change of venue!" Julia hesitated, having no idea where this 'change of venue' would spring from in the heart of the Texas desert.

As if by magic, the aircraft was spot on time. Not even a delay as an excuse for not arriving in time for their excursion. The onward journey of a lifetime Mark had expressed seemed more like the flight of the phoenix to Jess, with no way out but to eat your feet.

She had to smile as her wild imagination took over at the prospect of sharing a makeshift bed with Mark on the first night in an age under canvas. The smile she feared would wane the moment he made his first advance.

Remembering his last words as she agreed to the 'torment' (a blissful holiday, his version) of the passion he had saved for their 'encounter', her mind strayed to Trevor Howard and Celia Johnson. The love was there, but Jess suspected it would be '*brief*'.

His smile as she alighted the aircraft at the Dallas Airport forced Jess to forget her doubts as to the purpose. Mark lifted her up and hugged her with every ounce of his Texan ability. "I've missed you so," his whispered affection, bringing to the fore the guilt she had harboured throughout the flight.

"Me too," she whispered, realising it to be almost true. No better words spoken than, "absence makes the heart grow fonder." They kissed passionately until they were exhausted.

The spread his housekeeper laid out was fit for a queen, not so the look in her eye as she eyed Jess with suspicion. "Welcome!" the word spoke without feeling. Jess had the distinct impression that getting past Wilhelmina would be a feat best dealt with later and on her own terms.

"Wilhelmina seems nice!" Jess smiled a false smile.

"She's very protective, but means well," Mark answered, hoping to quell Jess's obvious concern that she had a mountain to climb before passing his housekeeper's scrutiny.

Chapter Fourteen

The imagined agony of her Texan saddle recalled fourfold, as each evening a hot bath to soak away the rigours of the day turned into a dip in the nearest watering hole, saw Jess wish she was back with Julia and as far away from Mark as physically possible.

His attempt to reconcile her discomfort with a hand on her breast and a kiss on the back of her neck did nothing to encourage her enthusiasm to make love.

Even Mark with his creative imagination failed to kickstart her passion. Her comfy four-poster with the scent of Gautier instead of a hay mattress housing all types of vermin and the smell of cattle droppings, was well outside her comfort zone and did nothing to inspire her sexual appetite.

His attempts to satisfy her turned into a comic strip. Hands and bodies flaying to reconcile the sound of howling wolves versus rattling snakes, his heavy breathing and whispered age-old expletives hoping to stimulate her desire, only made matters worse.

"Was that good for you?" falling on deaf ears as Jess rearranged her dressing gown hoping to distract further attention.

"Of course, darling," came out of her mouth instead of, 'Good? it was bloody unbelievable!'

Trying to focus on the here and now instead of alighting the plane on the way back to New York, Jess spent her days pretending to enjoy the experience.

It became more and more obvious to Jess their compatibility had been purely sexual and not Mark's expectation that she would fall under the spell of his ranch with everything it entailed.

Far from it. She envisaged at the onset of their relationship being cosseted, wined and dined in the best New York had to offer, but this was a different ball game, one Jess had no intention of playing a moment longer than necessary.

The next 'treat' Jess suffered through was a jeep safari to see his latest oil well.

"We've had a new gusher over on the far side," Mark indicated with his hand. "One I know you'll want to see. Liquid gold they call it," he enthused, handing her a mask to keep out the dust.

Wilhelmina grinned, seeing Jess's discomfort. "Another one bites the dust," she whispered to herself, thinking Mark would see sense soon and realise she was not the one.

"Enjoy!" her parting grin said it all.

"You're welcome to him," Jess mumbled to herself as their jeep took off at speed.

Accompanied by uncouth rangers and oil men, instead as hoped, a life escorted by immaculate gents and ladies of fine breeding, visiting the high life in limousines, this was back to nature with a bump.

Literally, as it turned out. The track overland was a misery never experienced before and not one Jess intended to encounter again.

No wonder their love life dwindled. She had bruising and discomfort from overzealous drivers and a hike to reach a black oil-soaked hole. "Soon to reap millions," Mark excitedly explained, as Jess looked on in disbelief that he may consider her the slightest bit interested.

Relieved when it was time for home was an understatement. On the plane journey, just as elegant as his life in the wild had been opposite, a re-evaluation of her future was now her priority.

"Never again," her intention to remain in her comfort zone, Jess made a pact with the devil. "It will be a long time in hell before I return to that mad house," her first words to Julia following her return.

Julia listened while Jess rambled on about snakes, eating food from a tin plate tasting like shit, and nights feeling like a heifer being humped by an overzealous adolescent buffalo. Her description did nothing to entice Julia to join her on her next adventure despite the billions of gushing oil turning into dollars by the minute.

"You didn't enjoy the trip then?" Julia sarcastically grinned.

She shook her head, wet from being washed a million times. Her mouth full of toothpaste, a luxury.

"Enjoy? You must be kidding. It was a nightmare. One I have no intention of repeating!" Jess shook her head, pulling a face.

Julia continuing to taunt, "I take it you and Mark are re-evaluating your relationship?"

"And some. Wild horses won't get me back there again. His housekeeper was a female version of 'Attila the Hun'. She made it obvious I wasn't wanted. I think she had her sights set on Mark herself. She won't get in a fight with me over who washes his pants and socks!" Jess began to smile, finally seeing the funny side.

Donning her Gucci suit and high heels, having brushed her red hair until it shone, Jess sprayed her most expensive perfume and sighed, "I feel almost human!"

"I must say, you look more like your old self," Julia, still jesting, replied. "Where would you like to go? Dancing and eating out at the finest restaurants?"

"Anywhere that doesn't do beans from a bucket over a fire will suit me fine." Laughing, Jess slung her mink stole over her shoulder. "After you."

Many calls from Mark were untaken. Finally, an urgent telegram, "Have you arrived home, ok? Love Mark."

Looking worried, Chris knocked Jess's door, "The poor man is desperate. What's wrong with you?"

"It's a long story, one better untold. Explain I'm fine, just busy. Send a kiss." Jess looked down.

"Not from me, I hope. I don't like oil, only with garlic on my salad," Chris joked, having had chapter and verse from Julia.

Unable to hide her smirk despite the irony, Jess returned his quip, "I have aversion to oil in my bath after that encounter," she laughed, shuddering. "Over my dead body!"

Their cloak and dagger brothel began raking in millions. Feathers and diamante to tantalise, silk stockings held up by red and black suspender belts, the scene was set for a good time.

Chris at the door kept unwanted nosey neighbours at bay, only by request and invitation, the clientele was vetted carefully.

No shocks, as was their historic experience, only gents of fine character and wealth were welcome.

"No riff raff," Julia insisted as the faithful (or should that be unfaithful) paraded the luxurious carpets from the expensive lounges to a bar with a drinks menu to rival the Ritz, sporting prices to match. Elegant bedrooms and ensuites embracing roll top baths were perfumed to maximise arousal. They had it all.

Word of mouth, the fastest way to increase the eager and those wishing to learn the ways of the world, their business flourished, as did their bankroll. Jess and Julia became famous in an underworld of businessmen and the idle rich.

No need to marry and risk a hefty divorce settlement. Marry, if you will, a would-be faithful wife, and finding pleasure in a palace such as J&J's was much more satisfying. The word was out and Jess and Julia knew exactly how to play the market.

Dressed to kill, the pair mingled with the rich and famous. Tempted to partake of what some had to offer, good looks, physiques to rival Adonis, with sexual appetites to match the most virile, only the thought of being stereotyped as 'Madams' prevented them from joining in.

It was hard to resist the laughter and tales told by the girls of the unusual exploits of some adventurous males. But resist they did, until one day when the dwindling masses had disappeared, leaving just one young gent, who, having refused the best of the best, propositioned Jess.

"You fascinate me!" elbow on the bar, the guy had refused to leave until Jess arrived to throw him out.

"You don't me!" Jess replied. Having been at the short end of such remarks before, she indicated her bouncer to help evict the obnoxious intruder.

"Please, I mean it. I'm not your usual Joe. I have watched you from afar and I am fascinated by you. I'm Edward, by the way!" slightly inebriated, he held out a shaking hand.

"Well, Edward, the only part of you that fascinates me is why you would wish to be forcefully evicted by my extremely able-bodied employees?" Jess's quick retort hit home.

"Why would I risk being devoured by your rottweilers when I could have had any of your girls at the drop of a hat but instead save myself for you?"

Jess was unable to stifle a laugh, "Modest, as well as all your other obnoxious, obvious talents?" she looked him up and down.

"Touché! Can we begin again?" Edward insisted.

"I had no idea we'd started. On your way stud. I'm not interested," Jess lied. This handsome young man intrigued her.

Julia had spotted him several nights, not going upstairs with the tarts he had been offered, but chose, instead, to stare in Jess's direction like a love-struck puppy. "He has the hots for you!" she laughed, watching his attempts to catch Jess's eye.

Having pushed men to one side, not only physically but mentally, Jess remained stoic, "I have no intention of encouraging over-sexed, under-brained young wannabes wanting something they can't have!" Jess had waved a hand in dismissal without giving Edward a second glance.

Julia persisted as nights moved on, "I'm telling you, you have an ardent admirer. We'd have no business if all men carried on in that way." She grinned, encouraging Jess to check him out.

"What would I do with a simpering, love-struck halfwit? I have no interest in being a forerunner to his next conquest." Jess was adamant he was on the make. "I'll be the next headline. 'Older woman devours young hormonal male wishing to practise on a more mature female.' No chance. I've been there, got the T shirt!" She laughed, which she hadn't since Mark. She had been a nun in floozy's clothing just as the job required.

"There's one for each of us!" Julia insisted.

"Not for me, there isn't," Jess leaving it there, decided to smile sweetly and charge more for his drinks.

"How do people get drunk in this establishment?" Edward, the hanger on, questioned Jess. "Your prices are steep even for my bank balance!"

"We don't force our patrons to drink until drunk. On your way if our prices outweigh your ability to pay!" Jess couldn't help a smile as his face changed.

"You're mistaken if you think me a scrounger. I have wealth beyond your wildest dreams."

"I don't succumb to wild dreams. Spend your dollars elsewhere if you're unhappy!" Jess replied, curter than she intended.

"I only come for the view!" he looked into Jess's eyes.

"We have many here to quell your overactive hormones. I'm not for sale." She turned to walk away.

"I have no desire to purchase your services. I find you irresistible," he added, sounding sincere as he walked toward the door.

"Let's get one thing straight. I have no intention of getting tangled in a fight for you to grow up. You are welcome as a customer but nothing else." Jess was adamant he had growing pains.

"I'm old enough to know my own mind and my mind is set on you!" With that, Edward closed the door behind him.

It was days before Edward returned. Chris immediately, as instructed by Jess, hailed the attention of one of their most beautiful young ladies. "See he is satisfied with the service," he said, pointing out Edward who was, true to form, at the bar.

"Hi, big boy, fancy a good time?"

Chapter Fifteen

Having been told the story of how Edward stormed out, Jess became suspicious that there was more to him than met the eye.

Chris still insisted he had been checked out thoroughly and was a perfectly respectable, no misdemeanour guy with extremely rich parents. Other than his infatuation with Jess, Edward was squeaky clean.

Feeling they had missed something that could entrap their business agenda, Jess did her own research.

"Hi, Jimmy, is it possible to check out a guy named Edward Garcia, he lives on…?"

Having repeated the address given by Chris, Jimmy interrupted, "Are you kidding me? These people are in the Forbes. I don't need to check them out. You would have to be living on the moon not to know of these people. Their kid, Edward, is one of the richest in America. He went to the top university and drives a state-of-the-art Jensen FF. He wants for nothing. Why? What's up? Are you looking for a husband?" he joked.

"No, stupid, I have no need to lick boots. Just checking him out, that's all!"

"I don't have to snoop on this one. Their mansion is bigger than the White House," Jimmy, the detective, laughed.

"Ok, I get it. He's Mr Respectable! Thanks a lot, Jimmy." Jess closed the call wondering why a kid of his ilk would be visiting a brothel when he must have girls by the dozen hanging around.

"He must be a stalker!" Chris laughed. "Spotted you in the park and it was love at first sight!"

"I don't do the parks. I have my own on the doorstep," Jess joked but still felt uneasy.

***

No need for applications to renew their 'agency' licence, the registrar was a regular visitor to their establishment.

Politicians, judges, police chiefs all made up the regular attendees. Generals returning from the Vietnam War were welcomed, as were all high-ranking soldiers, airmen and seafaring captains when off duty.

Every male needing comfort in the arms of their sophisticated, well-groomed, multilingual ladies of the night was treated with the utmost discretion, not only for the participants' protection, but also for the good name of J&J's business venture.

Quite a feat you may think under the circumstances, but as everyone left feeling satisfied and happier than when they arrived, keeping the activities secret was far easier than Jess and Julia imagined.

Mutual respect for the other's privacy, ensured discretion on a level demanded of a doctor patient relationship or a priest in a confessional, their business grew with their clientele.

As their clandestine bordello grew in stature, their bank balance overflowed with wealth at an amazing rate.

Jess found the excitement intoxicating, a little like a drug or drink addict, only by looking, not partaking.

Julia and Jess made a solemn pact never to get involved with the clients, as to do so would endanger not only their business, but the trust valued highly by their participants.

It was like sworn secrecy during the war. One word out of place and their whole world, and that of their clients, would crumble and this was the last thing either party wanted.

J&J's themed nights were renowned within its community. Wild West whore nights, French can-can dancers, old English royalty evenings, garden parties late at night under the stars, horse riding during the day, all enjoyments ending upstairs for their patrons' titillation.

Edward's threat when Jess explained her position ended badly. "You will see I don't take rejection easily," he shouted, running towards his car.

A nod to Sandy, her bodyguard, and his keys were removed, preventing him from leaving due to drink and until she could calm him, saw a tantrum more befitting a teenager.

"My family will have your guts for garters." His fist in the air, he began to run down the drive.

"Look, son, the miss is sorry, all right. She has a partner who is extremely jealous and fears for your safety!" Sandy took his arm whilst trying to reason with him.

"Liar," Edward bawled, struggling to get free.

That's when the ethos changed completely. A fist in Sandy's face was returned with a push from the six foot four, 108kg trained boxer and Edward fell like a stone.

Jess ran to the scene, anxious for confirmation he was alright, "Will he be ok?" she whispered, seeing CPR being performed by Sandy with Chris on hand to help.

"I'm afraid not!" Chris said, feeling for a pulse.

"Oh, Christ. I didn't mean to hurt him," Sandy murmured, lifting Edward in his arms.

Fearing the worst for everyone, Chris gestured to the summer house. "Bring him in here. You go back inside and pretend this never happened," he spoke softly to Jess as Sandy looked on in shock.

Feeling the tension rise, Jess took Chris's arm. "Tell Julia I want to see her," she whispered. "And be quick!"

Julia's footsteps down the path as she ran to the scene stopped short of the door as she glanced inside. "What's happened? Is he drunk?" she asked Chris, seeing Edward spread eagle.

The look on Jess's face as Sandy struggled to straighten Edward's legs needed no reply. "Oh my God!

What are we to do?" Julia exclaimed, holding Jess's hand.

"I'll sort it," Sandy said, wishing he had a magic wand. "Go back inside and ask Josie to bring her bag of tricks!"

Jess and Julia, not asking questions, did as he asked. Seeing Josie sitting on a punter's knee, smiling sweetly as he propositioned her, Jess whispered the words, "Bag of tricks to the summer house." Signalling one of her other girls to take over, Josie moved stealthily as if in slow motion.

"What's up?" Josie questioned without blinking an eye.

"Sandy and Chris need your help!" Jess whispered, smiling a false smile towards their guests.

Pretending to mingle, the pair moved towards the garden, "Oh God, Julia, what are we to do? This will ruin us and others, not forgetting his parents." Jess, hysterical on the inside, but quietly calm on the outside, tried to take in the implications.

At first, Julia remained statue-like, then without further reflection, "Come on, Jess, we need to sort this out!" Taking Jess's hand, Julia purposefully made towards the summer house after checking they were alone.

Shocked beyond words, the pair watched as Josie took out a hypodermic needle and Sandy injected Edward with whatever was in it.

As he looked up, his face ashen, he turned to Josie, "Give me a minute. Wait for me on the patio." A finger to his lips signalled she remain silent.

Unable to speak, Julia thought she would faint. Jess was first to react as the words stumbled from her mouth, "What? What... was that?" she stuttered, pointing towards Edward and then to the needle as Julia looked on horrified.

"It's all we could think of," Sandy breathed heavily. "I'm hoping I injected the drug soon enough. It needs to circulate giving the impression it was self-induced." His sigh sounded animal-like as he gripped Edward's hand around the hypodermic.

Jess and Julia sat mortified as Chris explained they needed to move the body fast. "I've asked Sandy to drive Edward's car close to the trees over there." Pointing toward the rear of the summer house, he began lifting the body without success.

Moving instinctively, Julia and Jess took a leg each. Julia retching uncontrollably, the three struggled, finally dragging Edward's body onto a curtain and through the shrubs just as Sandy pulled up in Edward's car.

The girls looked on as Sandy collected Edward, still wrapped in the curtain and placed him carefully onto the back seat. "Go back to the house. I will take care of the rest!" he said, taking control of the situation as Chris and Jess stood motionless and Julia once more threw up.

Having spent the evening pretending to be part of the festivities, their acting abilities tested to the ultimate, the end of the night was a relief beyond words.

Sitting comatose on Jess's bed, she and Julia reflected. "That's the worst thing ever!" Julia first to speak, murmured, "I'm petrified!"

"Me too!" Jess replied, tears in her eyes as the horror of the night sunk in.

"What do you think will happen?" Julia asked, not having a clue how it would end.

The knock on the door made Jess jump. Thinking it may be the police, Julia asked, "Who is it?" in a voice as normal as possible, while Jess rushed to the bathroom to wash away her tears.

"It's only me!" the voice of Chris answered, sounding weird.

Jess rushed to the door, pulled it open and clung to Chris as if life itself depended upon it. Crying uncontrollably, Jess looked into his eyes, "What's happened?"

Having returned from meeting Sandy, the picture became more real as Chris explained, "Sandy drove to lover's pinnacle." Taking a breath, he continued, "He placed Edward's body face up over a rock a few feet down, making sure the damage caused when he was pushed made contact.

"He left Edward's car at the top with the door open." Trembling, Chris added, "The idea being, he was under the influence of drink and drugs, stepped out of his car, fell backwards and died at the scene." He sat down with a sigh. "We can only hope they believe it." He stuttered, "Sandy was very thorough, cleaning and clearing every sign he was there." He lifted crossed fingers.

Julia spoke first, "It was an accident. We should have informed the police!"

"The high brass police were here, remember?" Chris emphasised, rubbing his temples.

Jess sat, trying to inwardly digest the bigger picture. "Not only that but our business would be outed, with a prison sentence for Sandy a surety and for us for breaking the regulations, not forgetting the permanent closure of everything we have strived for."

They stopped a moment to reflect. "All for the sake of a crazy kid!" Chris rationalised.

"Do you think his parents know he visits a brothel?" Julia said with a stricken face.

A grimace with the harrowing situation, Jess replied, "Do you really think he would tell them? His pals maybe, but his parents, I think not!"

"What if his pals tell?" Trying to resolve every scenario, Julia couldn't stop poking the sore.

"Unlikely? Why would they explain his sexual desires?" Chris, knowing more of male secrecy pacts, questioned.

Julia shook her head weakly, hoping all the ends had been tied up. How to move forward with the knowledge was a different story.

Chapter Sixteen

A sobbing mother and an enraged father stood before the camaras outside the coroner's court. "My son didn't do drugs!" he insisted, anger and sadness in his eyes.

Hands shot up, "Many parents are kept in the dark!" The microphone pressed forward for his reply was hastily moved by Edward's father's bodyguards.

"No," he insisted, gesturing to his guards to stand down. "I want the world to know this is not who my son was. He was an intelligent, informed person who stood up to the people promoting drugs. Something stinks and I intend to throw as much weight and dollars as needed to discover the truth." With that, he took hold of his broken wife's hand and took the steps into a life without his only son.

Seeing the televised interview, Julia and Jess could no longer hold their composure. "I feel like shit!" Jess wailed, tears streaming down her face.

"I wish he hadn't been so stupid. Why would a young, great looking guy like Edward feel the need to visit our business? It makes no sense," Julia added, a deep sigh indicating her despair.

Feeling in some way responsible, Jess sobbed, "How can we answer a question that no one, least of all me, has the slightest idea of? It's a mystery." She hesitated, feeling devastated for Edward's family. "How many onwards and upwards does one person have to encounter?" Jess said, thinking 'why her'.

"You're a survivor! The past is proof of that. We'll find a way through this together," Julia put a comforting arm around Jess's shoulder.

"Maybe, maybe not!" Jess, thinking of leaving the country to start afresh, shrunk lower into her chair.

"A brothel on the coast of somewhere hot and sticky?" Julia tried to lighten the deep sorrow they were experiencing.

***

The tickets arrived, not for a permanent move, just a long holiday, leaving Chris to work his magic after the frenzy and speculation surrounding Edward's death.

A catamaran trip around the Island of St. Lucia seemed the answer. More rum punch than the most ardent drinkers could hold, music louder, dancing to the rhythm of the Caribbean, the party began as the sun set.

Julia, feeling the need to join the shakers and movers, held Jess's hand. The rum did the trick and Jess moved in time with the music. The benefit of the atmosphere, singing a duet with a stranger, set the scene for a night of recovery.

Laughing, Jess and the stranger moved in unison. It was obvious he was a natural on the dance floor. Responding as she had been trained, Jess relaxed and let down her hair. "Thank you, kind sir," she smiled a smile that had intoxicated many men, including Edward, whose dead body remained in her brain.

"My pleasure!" His voice accented just enough to reveal his birth country.

Jess was unable to resist using her talent for discovering a person's origins when enlisting wealthy clients. "English, isn't it?" she lifted her head, meeting his eyes full on.

"Clever girl. I was hoping to have adopted my chosen country's accent by now!"

He smiled an intoxicating smile. "I'm Jessica. Pleased to meet you." *Will you never learn?* she asked herself, feeling the need to flirt.

He held her hand longer than necessary before replying, "I'm Sebastian. Bas to my friends and yes, I'm from London originally," he added, not giving away his adopted home.

"Well, Sebastian, I hope to gain the right to call you Bas!" Jess, looking over the top of her glass, sipped the cocktail. "I'm American, as if I need to elaborate, and it's Jess to my friends!" she laughed, knowing her accent was unmistakable.

The Pitons to the left, open sea to the right, the captain sailed leisurely into the sunset.

Those not having experienced the phenomenon made their way to the upper deck. The more familiar, as were Julia and Jess, stayed to watch the dolphins as they frolicked, reflecting brilliant colours in the sea.

It was hard to imagine a more beautiful place. Although they were frequent visitors to the Caribbean, somehow, after the trauma of recent months, everything seemed more real.

The singing, more out of tune as the rum and headiness of the evening took hold, was acceptable to even the more conservative audience.

"Inspiring," Julia announced as the steel drums played familiar tunes.

"Care to dance?" Sebastian, outstretched hand and a suntanned smile, once again requested of Jess.

Julia lifted an eyebrow. No need for words. Her look of expectation said it all.

"Thank you, I'd be delighted," Jess replied, his gaze unable to be broken.

The slower the music, the closer he held her. Not as expected, the fervour of anticipated sex, but a gentle, more romantic warmth as his arms enfolded her scantily clad frame.

Looking down as she looked up, it was obvious that something was happening, "What's going on, Jess?" his question, unable to be answered, as Jess moved closer, responding to his bodily reaction.

Finally, the music stopped and the chef announced, "Supper is served."

Sebastian smiled and stood, holding Jess in his arms. "I fear my hunger is for more than exotic food," he whispered.

Not wanting to tempt fate, as had been her downfall before, but unable to resist, Jess replied, "I'm also starving. Shall we partake?" Her innuendo was loaded as they moved toward a table set for kings. A king-size bed crossed the old Jess's mind. Had this been another time and place and not on a boat full of marauding tourists, Jess felt sure things would be different.

A hand on her bare back, an unmistakable and unexpected shiver passed through Jess's overheated body as a desire to kiss him and more overwhelmed her.

A slight cough, a shake of the head and Jess smiled. Had this been a hotel instead of a boat, she would have uttered, "Your room or mine?" As it was, she offered Sebastian a glass of champagne with a promise to herself to take things slowly.

No more the impulse of old, she knew nothing of the man that took her breath. Logic told her all men were the same, a holiday romance following too many drinks, moving on to the next easy catch the following day. Jess had no intention of being the reject.

Julia, seeing their body language, was eager to hear her friend's confession. She was disappointed when Jess smiled sweetly, "A possible maybe!" She ate her seafood salad as if the encounter hadn't happened.

"He seems very nice," Julia exclaimed, expecting chapter and verse.

"Nice is for cream cakes," Jess joked, seeing a plate full of her favourites.

It was obvious no explanation would be forthcoming, so Julia settled in for a night without her friend. Not so! Sebastian left Jess at her hotel door having wandered in from the gardens. His warm goodnight kiss found her tongue, stirring her sexual appetite like no other had so far achieved.

"See you tomorrow?" his whispered. "Au revoir," set the scene for another encounter.

"Well, what's the verdict?" Julia questioned, not having fallen asleep wondering if Jess was ok.

"He's not married and he has a successful business as a photographer here in the Caribbean. His family are wealthy farmers," she hesitated. "And no, he's not a rancher. He has a brother who will take over the farm on his father's demise," Jess laughed, thinking no more riding the plains for her. "And he is not a letch!"

"You mean you didn't???" Julia began to laugh, thinking he must bat for the other side.

"No and no. He's very manly, attentive but not overly so. I felt safe in his company if that's your meaning!"

"He didn't try to seduce you?"

"Julia! Honestly, we hardly know each other," Jess lied feigning innocence. "He certainly has no idea I'm a partner in a brothel." As Jess said the words, she realised her profession would certainly not endear her new friend or his family should their relationship progress.

"It's fine if it's just a holiday romance!" Julia hesitated, looking for signs Jess hadn't fallen hard.

"Hmm, I will have to give that some thought. For now, I'm enjoying the attention," Jess replied, unsure how to react.

Although she didn't elaborate, Julia, knowing her friend well, was concerned. Her own relationships had nose-dived when her prospective others had learned of her vocation. It seemed the pair were destined to casual acquaintances and not the all-consuming love of a settled relationship.

It hadn't crossed Jess's mind of the consequences should she fall in love. Her experiences so far were dictated by the need to improve her status-quo. *Love*, she scoffed to herself, *is for dreamers and writers with vivid imaginations.* It hadn't occurred to her until now that the 'real thing' may be possible.

Jess had considered love to be what she and Mark had shared. Looking back, it was doomed from the start. Her initial intention to trap him into a marriage of convenience had turned to more, knowing now lust had played a major roll whilst compatibility was found wanting. The reality of a lifelong partnership with him or anyone seemed remote.

After exchanging telephone numbers, it was time to part. The romance of the island, warm sun and tender lovemaking with Sebastian in another life where her background and ambition weren't an issue, a long-term commitment may have been possible.

Leaving St Lucia with memories of a holiday romance a pleasant distraction, Jess settled in for the long haul. Hoping the dust had settled with Edward's family suitably convinced he had committed suicide, Jess hoped their arrival back in the US would be back to normal.

"Do you think you will see him again?" Julia asked with a questioning look.

Jess playing the innocent, casually replied, "Who? If you mean Sebastian, I wouldn't think so. He's sure to have many more respectable suitors."

Julia didn't comment. She was only too aware that their profession (if you could call it that) would deter most eligible bachelors. Likewise, married men with baggage were out of the question. Divorced? There must be a valid reason for the decision. It was a minefield neither wished to tread.

Casual sex or flirtations were the only way forward for the owners of J&J. Acceptance that their future was dictated by the past made true love an option neither considered.

The mansion lit up, music drifted into the night air as their limousine approached. "Good evening. It's great to have you back." The voice of Desmond's welcome was heart-warming.

"It's good to be back," the pair chorused, happy in their comfort zone.

The raucous welcome took them by surprise. Hand shaking and smiles from their clients, hugs and cheek kissing from Chris and Howard, coats taken, drinks in hand, it was as if they'd never been away.

Tails wagging, running around as if demented, their dogs, Diesel and Jeremy, jumped up, licking their faces, responding to kisses from Jess and Julia. It was great to be back.

Chapter Seventeen

The newspapers saved by Chris were full of harrowing news. A ransom as if a king, Edward's father spared no dollar. The outcome, a harassed inspector as every crank and socially inept individual confirmed they knew the answer.

Pleading for an end to his interference saw despair replace anger as Edward's father failed to come to terms with the inevitable.

Their last-ditch attempt to convince the tabloid press that the police had it wrong ended with the exchange of millions of dollars and the disappearance of the blackmailer. Nothing, as far as Jess could discover, had happened since.

"All quiet on the western front!" Chris confirmed, feeling confident their plan had worked.

Sandy, a sceptic, suggested they wait for the dust to settle. "It may take an age for his family to accept he caused his own death. In their eyes, their whiter-than-white son will never fall from grace."

Despite the case being closed and the funeral over, Sandy still harboured feelings they were being too complacent.

The surprise for Jess was an unrecognised letter. Thinking it from the police or a mistake, she took a double take at the envelope.

Confirming her address, the content read, *"My dear Jess, I realise this letter will come as a surprise. Reflecting on our time together had an impact on me like never before. I'm not a poet or a man of fine words, so forgive me if I stumble when trying to explain.*

I have experienced many liaisons, of which some have had possibilities for more a meaningful relationship, but none greater than my meeting up with you.

I feel the need to write and hope you realise this letter is not one of flippancy, but are words not spoken by me before.

My psychological attachment to you has not wavered since we parted. No stronger draw for one person to another has impacted so greatly, preventing sleep and concentration.

Normally, I'm a balanced and logical man. Therefore, my continued feelings for you begs the question, do you feel the same?

Love Sebastian (Bryce-Parks)"

Having read his letter a third time, Jess had no idea how to respond. This was a first from a man she found profoundly disturbing, with his words reflecting her own uncanny. In a different life, she would have gladly extended a hand across the sea to discover if Sebastian could be the one, but her reservations should he discover her lifestyle, would greatly affect her reply.

She sought out Julia, hoping she may help, although how anyone could was a mystery. A woman of two virtues, one having sought a better life at any cost, the other desperate for the love of a man that understood her, it was a quandary unable to be unravelled.

Jess doubted there was an answer. Sebastian or any other man would find her position difficult to come to terms with.

Edward, with his warped ideology of what a good wife would be, was a typical example. His obsession had ended badly and Jess had no intention of reliving the experience.

Mark, with his oil wells and incompatible lifestyle, had taught her a lesson not to be repeated.

Sebastian's endearing persona, wonderful smile and gentle manner had been the nearest to her expectations. Jess had no doubt that at a different time and a different place, he would be the one.

Julia, rolling up her sleeves, smiled, seeing her friend staring through the window, deep in thought. "Turned to stargazing, have we? Or are you looking for the meaning of life?" she joked until Jess spun around, tears in her eyes. "Are you ok?" Julia added, placing a comforting arm around her shoulder.

"Nothing that rubbing out my life so far wouldn't solve!" she wiped a silent tear.

"I'm not sure I understand?" a bewildered reply as the last time Julia had spoken to Jess, she was reminiscing about her wonderful holiday.

Taking a moment before handing Julia the letter, Jess replied, "I feel the same, but there's nothing I can do about it!"

Carefully reading each word, Julia wasn't surprised. "It seems my intuition was right!" she murmured, shaking her head.

"You mean you knew what was happening?" Jess replied.

"Not the detail, but the look in your and Sebastian's eyes said it all," hesitating, Julia realising the obstacles, added, "Maybe an honest answer leaving nothing out would test the water for a solution?"

"I do share his feelings. I'm sure of that. Equally, our business choice would seal my fate. If not with him, I'm sure his family and friends wouldn't be ecstatic, knowing his fiancée is a madam," Jess whispered.

"Not the best profession for a stable and loving family life, I must confess. But who knows what his line of work is. He may be a bank robber or drug pusher in his spare time." Julia tried to coax her to reply just in case.

"He's a photographer, for Christ's sake. He takes pictures and sells them for a living, not exactly Al Capone!" Jess started to cry.

"I'm sorry, Jess. Would you like to dissolve our partnership?" Julia was saddened by the prospect but asked anyway.

Faced with a fait accompli, Jess had no answer. Would it be too much to sacrifice for something unknown, or would it end happily ever after?

"Why does my life always end in a quandary? Is it, isn't it, or will it, won't it? There's always a stumbling block." She thought how easy it must have been for her parents, but then she remembered every relationship has a downside.

"Confess it all, you love him but…. Say it as it is and it's down to him!" Julia said, seeing no other way.

They sat at the typewriter and began. "*Dear Sebastian, Before I confess my undying love, I have many things to explain….*" Jess stopped, "Things? How do I explain I'm a brothel owner?" She sat head in hands.

Clearly seeing the dilemma, Julia replied, "Try explaining from the beginning. It may be easier!"

"Easier? My life has been one disaster after another, not forgetting covering up a murder."

"Ouch!" Julia exclaimed. "When you put it like that, perhaps a little smoothing over the edges would be best."

Feeling a smirk coming on, more from anxiety, Jess was unable to resist, "Why don't I confess, go to jail, do my time and when I come out, finish this letter?" Unable to control a tearful grin, Jess sank in a chair as the pair cried and laughed. "It would be easier to tell him a complete lie. It would probably be more believable."

"True!" Julia remonstrated, turning serious. "Let's begin again!"

Dear Sebastian…. "Well, that's a start," Julia said as the pair tried to control the urge to scream.

"At least he knows he's 'dear'!" Jess sadly joked. "Let's get a drink. Maybe when I'm drunk, I will think of something feasible?"

After her third, "In the face of adversity…." Jess slurred, "The enemy back tracked and ran for the woods!"

"What's that got to do with anything?" Julia looked over the top of her glass.

"That's what I'd do if I was faced with me!!" Jess drunkenly winked.

"You're not his enemy!"

"That's not how his family will see it!" Taking another drink, Jess hoped the burn would deaden her nerves.

A heap of screwed up paper overflowed the waste basket. "Do you think when we're sober would be best?" Julia finally asked, eyes half shut with nothing more to type.

"Maybe if I try typing and you dictate?" Jess slithered from the couch onto the typist chair.

Dear Sebastian…. Jess typed before sobbing uncontrollably.

"Time for bed," Julia whispered, sobering up with Jess's despair.

A quick note, *"Dear Sebastian, give me a little time and I will be in touch. Jessica."* No love and kisses, Jess mounted the stairs held up by Julia.

A knock on the door saw Jess focus on the clock. Midday and still her eyes were blurred. "Just a minute," she held her head trying to find her way to the door.

Through the peephole, Chris was smiling, "It's only me. Just wondered if you were coming down for brunch?"

Opening the door gingerly, Jess confessed, "Don't mention food. I'll never be hungry again."

"Oh dear, you do look a sorry sight. I assume you've forgotten the meeting with the municipality after lunch?"

Trying to focus, Jess sat down with a bump. "What meeting?"

"To discuss an extension to your future business use. It's extremely important we show solidarity if you expect the committee to sign it off for another five years," Chris explained, thinking never in this world will she be up to it!

"Give me half an hour and I'll be ready!" Jess replied. "Is Julia prepared?"

"I've done all the spade work. All you and Julia have to do is show up looking like businesswomen of some standing." He stared at Jess as she tried to take off her dressing gown. "Standing would be good here!" he smiled, seeing how difficult that would be.

"Fear not, I have a solution!" she took out a remedy for drunken sots.

True to form, Julia and Jess came down the stairs just as Desmond opened the door. Sandy approached with the limousine. "Make it smart," Chris said, closing the door, hoping the pair would cut muster.

An endearing smile towards the court's chief clerk, a familiar face in their bordello, Jess began to speak as if a miracle had happened. "Registrar, we have met many challenges this year and thanks to my partner and our professional team, we have successfully achieved our goals. Not only in the education of the young, but our business has remained financially viable." She hesitated as Julia came to the fore.

"With your leave," she nodded to the bench, "we wish to report the consistent gratitude received from the families of our clients." Julia held up paperwork containing made up platitudes.

The documents previously suggested by the registrar were handed to the clerk. Flipping through, as if the first time he had seen them, he smiled, "Everything seems in order." Handing them back, nodding his approval, the registrar signed the five-year extension without looking up. "Next."

Chapter Eighteen

Deciding not to celebrate on this occasion, the three made their way to the local library. "I have some research to do. It won't take long!" Jess said, sending Chris back without them.

Following last night's fiasco, they entered the library. Jess looked up Sebastian's family name. "Let me see." She removed the envelope. His name and address for a reply clearly stated Sebastian Bryce-Parks. "Hmm, Bryce-Parks, there can't too be many with a name like that!"

Flipping through an English genealogy microfiche reader to the 'B's, it didn't take long for the name Bryce to appear. Bryce hyphen Parks took a little longer. "There's only a few. His family's ancestral tree should give us the answer," she whispered as Julia looked on.

Checking for 'Sebastian' Bryce-Parks was a challenge. Jess was just about to say, "Do you think he changed his forename?" when third from last, his first and family name appeared.

"Six?" Julia questioned, "He has five siblings? That's one big family."

"The more siblings, the more obstacles for me to overcome. Just imagine, I will not only have to convince his parents, but five brothers or sisters?" Jess shook her head in despair.

"It's impossible to know until you try," Julia realised Jess was right to question her chances. "You mentioned he was estranged from his family, as he relinquished his right to the family farm. Maybe they won't care who he marries."

"And how do you suggest I discover that?" Jess, losing the will to live with all the stumbling blocks, murmured.

"Dear Sebastian,
I would like to invite you to my home. I run my business from the same address so feel free to speak to my secretary, Chris, to make sure I'm available before you start out. Look forward to seeing you.
Love Jess. Xx"

"Have you lost the plot?" Julia was shocked as she looked over her shoulder.

"Take the 'bull by the horns' and watch the fur fly!" Jess said, licking the glue on the envelope. Placing it in the out tray, she flounced from the office.

"And your intention when he arrives?" Julia was fascinated by a side to Jess she hadn't encountered before.

"That, my dear Julia, will be down to him! I am who I am and for once, I will hold nothing back. If he turns and runs, then I have my answer. If he stays and accepts me, then the same applies."

Julia, thinking Jess had thrown her dummy out, smiled a knowing smile, "If this is bravado, I hope you know what you're doing?"

"I have no choice. All the ifs and buts will get me nowhere, so going for broke will sort it out once and for all."

Seeing Chris gather up the post, Jess's heart flipped. Knowing deep down that her actions were right didn't stop the anguish. No use fingers crossed, this wasn't a fairy tale. It was her life and it could turn out either way.

Reflecting on her mom's teachings, *you will know when the right one comes along*, Jess felt sure Sebastian was the one. How he would react when faced with her reality, she had no idea.

Sitting in an armchair, a high back studded in leather depicting an era of wealth and comfortable living, she began imagining Sebastian by her side. A tall good-looking man with a physique to die for, he would fit in well. All the girls would flutter around him, but knowing he was hers would deter even the most adventurous.

Jess quite liked the idea of a strong man helping run the business. It hadn't occurred to her to mention to Julia the implications his acceptance may involve.

It's possible Julia would object to a third person on their contract but felt sure they could work something out.

"Daydreaming?" Chris asked, "This guy under your skin?"

"Too many questions and no answers," Jess replied, not wishing to go into detail.

Chris, guessing the dilemma, called back over his shoulder, "He'll be a fool if he doesn't snap you up. If he wants a reference, I'd be happy to oblige." Chris pondering the outcome, smiled.

Jess blew an air kiss as Chris moved to the door to welcome the early arrivals. "This way," he smiled, "I have just the person to make your night." His easy manner and gentle persona encouraged even the most naïve.

What would we do without him? Jess wondered, hoping he and Sebastian, should he stay, would become friends.

The dice were thrown and how they fell was the million-dollar question. Awaiting the outcome was like walking over hot coals, but, nevertheless, Jess had a business to run and she continued as if nothing had happened.

Making way through the throng of revellers, the evenings excited her. Equally, the daytime strolls with her dogs calmed her. All that was missing was the passion of a strong, virile male to tantalise and satisfy her.

Jess daydreamed of Sebastian. Remembering the hotel room in St Lucia where he removed her negligée, slowly kissing her breasts, his tongue lingering down her body, raising her to heights unknown before. His foreplay was carefully executed with precision until she begged for more. It was as if life had only just begun as he touched her, first gently, then as if life itself depended upon it. The overwhelming passion released at the same time made Jess shudder as the memories rushed back with a vengeance.

The call from Julia brought her down to earth, "Jess, the clients are leaving. Clinton won't go home without saying goodnight!"

"Tell him I'll be right there," she replied as she wondered how Sebastian would respond to these overzealous, over-sexed individuals who fawned over her.

If she hadn't been so busy, Jess would have worried. No reply to her invitation had arrived and she wondered if it ever would. A million reasons passed her mind, ending with the assumption he had lied and was happily married.

Trying to dismiss the feelings of being used, she began making plans to move the summer house to another position in the garden. Since the unhappy demise of Edward, it had remained locked with no one setting foot through the door.

It had been a beautiful sanctuary, but one they all agreed had lost its allure. No more the warm atmosphere during colder days or the pleasure of flowers in summer adorning every space. It was now a reminder of torment and sadness and Jess wanted to obliterate the memories, not the ambience of a bygone age.

"This will have to be done very carefully," she instructed Howard, who had no idea why she had taken the decision.

Shaking his head, he said, "It's a perfect position where it is. Trees to shelter the midday sun and protection from the severe frosts in winter. What is there not to like?"

His question was unable to be answered as Jess agreed entirely. Had it not been such a tragedy, she would have confided in him in an instant.

"I thought a further greenhouse for exotic plants in its place. Many who seek refuge in your garden would appreciate another area to enjoy the fruits of your labour. It may also be a good place to educate your trainees."

Howard, not wishing to override Jess's thinking, shook his head. "Perhaps I could grow and display them in there!" he signalled with his hand to the rear of the summerhouse where Edward had lain dead.

Jess had to think quick, "I had considered a small café to the back of a new greenhouse with a place to relax in the main body. This move would cover all options," she adlibbed.

Still unsure, but resigned to the idea, "Who do you propose we employ to dismantle and re-erect the old place?" Howard questioned.

"Under your supervision, I thought the same builders who restored the mansion. They were extremely knowledgeable of how our ancestors completed their tasks." Jess once more tried to cover her tracks.

Not wanting to dispute the wishes of Jess, Howard looked toward the lake. "Was your thinking to overlook the lake?" he asked, not sure where would be a better option.

"Yes, close to the walled garden, but not too close as to overshadow the beautiful work you have carried out so far." Jess tried to smooth the way for something she realised Howard had no stomach for.

"Hmm, it may work!" he finally agreed. "I will call the builders today for their opinion as to how we begin and the cost."

Always mindful of the balance between practicalities and cost, Howard viewed the possibilities. Reservations that it would deflect the beauty and design by dismantling and re-modelling with consideration of the sunrise and sunset, he tried to open his mind to the changes.

Walking back together, they remained quiet. "What is it, Jess? I feel there is more to this change than you've expressed?" Howard finally asked.

Not wishing to explain the real reason, Jess hesitated. "Julia and I have realised the worth of a more diverse environment for our clients. The garden you have already so expertly transformed would be put to its best advantage. A coffee shop, giving another option to chat and get to know each other, should they not wish to indulge in our other amenities, seems a perfect solution."

Julia would be proud of me, Jess thought, thinking it an acceptable reason.

"When you put it like that…!" Howard smiled, squeezing her hand as he nodded his approval.

"I think I sold it to him!" Jess relayed her findings.

Julia smiled, "A coffee shop? What next? A sunken fish tank to stare at should they not gel with their chosen partner, akin to watching paint dry?" she joked.

Replying as Chris walked in, Jess grinned, "It was all I could think of at the time."

"What this time?" Chris asked, curious to discover their latest whiz.

Having explained, it was obvious Chris was uncertain. "What if the whole thing crumbles the moment the first part is moved?" he asked, looking under his eyes.

Hesitating, Julia replied, "Then the solution will be decided by a visit to the dump!"

Chapter Nineteen

One eye on the post and the other on the builders as they patrolled the summer house for the thousandth time, Jess wondered if either would end satisfactorily.

Unable to control the dilemma, she resigned herself to the inevitable. Both could spectacularly crash and burn or end in a happy resolution. The former, to convince Sebastian all wasn't as it seemed, would be an upward struggle, but one Jess intended to give her best shot. The latter, the extortionate cost of moving the summer house, but dollars Julia and Jess were prepared to sacrifice.

Having been informed by the builder no guarantees could be given, the pair stood open-mouthed as the cranes and scaffold began to arrive.

"OMG!" Julia exclaimed as the weight of the cranes destroyed a large part of the pristine lawn Howard had spent hours perfecting.

Tears in her eyes, Jess watched in horror as the trampling of dozens of boots over his flower beds became almost too much to bear. That and no reply from Sebastian forced a sob as she ran from the scene.

Burying her head in a pillow, Jess's resolve waned. The longer it took for Sebastian to reply, the more her plans seemed doomed to the trashcan.

The sound of breaking glass did nothing to ease her distress. The shouting, "Stop!" saw everything come to a halt as part of the end section of the conservatory fell with a crash to the ground.

"Luckily," the builder began to reassure them, "the frame is still intact. We have suppliers that collect antique glass and I feel sure they will come up with replacements."

Despite his encouraging words, Julia and Jess were in shock at the sight of the beautiful masterpiece in bits despite the tragic memories.

"Thank you," was all Julia could manage as the pair turned and made for the bar.

"Set 'em up!" Jess said as their barman looked on, thinking the end of the world was in sight.

"Make them a double," Julia added, feeling the pressure of their decision.

Taking the first down in one, Jess pushed her glass forward for a refill. "What next in the J&J scenario?" she questioned, feeling the burn of alcohol.

"Only a crystal ball can tell us that!" Julia answered, nodding to the barman for a third.

"No use crying in your soup!" A word from Chris forced the pair to look up. "I have every confidence in the builders. They have assured me they will have it back to its former glory before you know it!"

"Hmm and how is he with broken hearts?" Jess, feeling inebriated, sighed.

Not having had one himself, Chris shook his head. "I'm the wrong one to ask, but I'm sure drinking won't solve it."

Days passed and the site was a quagmire. Nothing could persuade Jess to visit as she continued to blame herself.

All the hard work of many men as they arrived, encountered a problem, and returned days after with the solution, was overseen by Chris and Howard, who were quietly confident all would be well in the end.

Days turned to weeks as the builders struggled to piece together the jigsaw that was once an outstanding showpiece of glass architecture.

Never losing sight of the progress made over the years by the invention of machinery, it was difficult to believe the original had been erected by hand. Nevertheless, the result was the same with the patting of backs and whispers of "Brilliant job," which saw the end of the project with praises for everyone taking part.

Unable to believe their eyes, Jess and Julia were overwhelmed. "I am astounded," Jess murmured. "In fact, I like it better over here," she added, walking the perimeter, checking the replaced glass.

Shaking hands with the 'magicians', as Julia called them, the pair turned to Howard. "Hire more men, if you wish, to sort out the garden," thinking a miracle or more would be needed.

"It's fine. I have many trainees that are up to the job," he replied, confident his teachings had been learned well. "It will give me the opportunity to design new flower beds and reorganise areas I've long wanted to change." He turned to Jess, "Subject to your approval, of course?"

"Dear Howard, you don't need our approval. You are the master of the garden, so do as you will. I'm sure we'll be happy with whatever you do." Jess squeezed his hand. "I wish my other problem was solved," Jess whispered under breath, sad once more, wondering why Sebastian hadn't replied.

Trying to put her personal woes to one side, Jess took pleasure in watching as Howard and his team restored and replenished the lawns and gardens to their former glory.

Having been given carte blanche with the design, Howard exceeded their wildest dreams. A stream meandering through a carefully stocked wildflower garden was a sensation.

"Twofold," was how Howard explained it. "Carp will flourish amongst their natural environment which has also been designed to attract bees, butterflies, dragon flies and many more species needing protection. I have planted a weeping willow tree just over there. This will grow and hang beautifully over the water near the half-moon bridge." Gestating with his hands, Howard continued to explain, "It will be especially attractive when the lights come on automatically each evening." His smile said it all.

"It's wonderful. What a genius you are," Jess romanced.

"Don't forget the budding gardeners. Without their help, this wouldn't have been possible," he returned her affection with a hug.

Julia back from her walk across the bridge, said, "Everyone will love the view of the house from the conservatory. It's magical," she romanced, an arm around Howard's shoulder.

"Steady on, you'll make me blush," he replied in an accent still difficult to understand.

Having thanked and congratulated his helpers, a substantial bonus for all was agreed. "We can't thank you all enough," Julia and Jess agreed, making their way inside the conservatory with Chris, hoping the bad memories had faded.

A complete transformation awaited them. "This way," Chris pointed to the botanical garden area, complete with a lemon tree and bougainvillaea draping the ceiling giving a tropical feel.

"And over here is where our clients will be given the opportunity to purchase flower arrangements for their wives and girlfriends," he grinned. "Not forgetting our full range of potting plants."

Howard began explaining the populous idea, hoping to make money. "This will not only cover the ongoing costs with any additional revenue from the café, but we also hope to support local charities," he added, feeling proud everyone would benefit.

The opening day arrived with a steady stream of clients, not only to sample the delights upstairs, but to take part in the splendid opening of the J&J arboretum.

Golf buggies arranged for the convenience of the not so agile, pathways lit up for the strollers, combined with the already secluded arbours for clients to discover their partner's preference, it was set to be a night to remember.

"Jess, can you spare a moment?" Chris left the guests as Jess and Julia alighted the stairs.

"Sure, what's up?" Jess thought an awkward guest or a hiccup in the kitchen was the problem.

"I have something for you!" he handed Jess a letter.

"I will deal with the bills in the morni...," she hesitated, seeing the handwritten envelope.

Jess stood statue-like as Chris pretended he had no idea who it was from. "Ok," he said casually, turning to take back the letter.

Holding it tight, she resisted, "I think....!" She tore open the envelope. "It's from Sebastian!" Her knees went weak.

"You asked him to make contact. Well, here it is." Chris smiled, having had Sebastian's call.

"Shame on you, Chris. How long have you known?"

"Early this morning. You were busy when I tried to explain."

Half wanting to read the letter, half not, Jess opened her eyes,

"Arriving on the twenty fifth. Flight details are below. Hope you can collect me from the airport. I have no idea where I am over there. Love Sebastian. X"

"What date is it again?" Jess looked frantic, hoping she had time to prepare.

"Sorry," Chris smiled. "It's today!"

"OMG! Where's Julia? I need to see her right away!"

Checking her image in the mirror, Jess was happy it was a mid-day touch-down. "How do I look?" she asked Julia, hoping her hair was in place.

"You look great. Go girl, let him see what he's been missing," Julia, only half convinced the decision Jess had made to throw herself under a bus from the onset was the wisest, stood fingers crossed behind her back.

"Now or never!" Jess replied, taking her Mustang convertible from the garage.

"No chauffeur-driven limo today?" Chris smiled.

"I don't want him to think I'm spoilt!" Jess laughed. Her hand in the air, she waved and spun down the drive and out onto the road.

Where this trip would lead, she had no idea.

Chapter Twenty

Jess was pacing, reading, and rereading the flight information board for the millionth time. *Why today a delay?* Jess psyched herself up with each announcement. It would be tougher than she thought, remembering her lines whilst wanting to hold him close.

Explaining her business would be the worst experience of her life. How he would react to her and Julia running a brothel was anyone's guess. Worse still was convincing him she was a custodian and not a participant.

Having practiced until word perfect, Jess was convinced until now that she could win him over and moving forward, he would see it was a business like any other.

The longer the delay, the more unsure she became she could pull it off. Repeating the words over and over until the announcement, "Flight 368 from Barbados is landing," the script left her mind and how much she loved him came to the forefront.

His smile when he spotted her amongst the other passengers took her breath. Arms outstretched, their bodies entwined, answering her questions with kisses, Sebastian, sun tanned, tall and extremely handsome, was everything she had longed for.

Tousled hair, unseeing eyes other than for each other, it was difficult to resist even in the mass of pushing and shoving holiday makers.

Clutching hands, embracing each other, they made for the parking lot. Sebastian looked shocked as they approached the convertible Mustang, more so as Jess placed the key in the lock.

This is Hollywood big style, he thought, loading his meagre crumpled leather holdall in the boot. *It's fancy, that's for sure,* he smiled to himself.

"Holding out on me, are you?" he grinned, kissing her passionately.

"This is only the beginning," she uttered, seeing the lovelight in his eyes. "All will be revealed," she smiled, a double meaning hoping to distract him.

Sexily, he smiled back, stopping her heart as they shared another passionate kiss. "I can't wait!" he mumbled, his arousal uncomfortable as they began the journey.

"I have something to show you." Teasing once more, she pulled the car to a halt overlooking the most spectacular view.

"I have everything I wish to see right here," he answered, nibbling her ear.

Following a lovemaking like no other, Jess sat upright. "Ok, here we go!" she said to Sebastian's surprise.

"So soon! I may need a few moments to recover!" he laughed until he saw the serious look on her face.

"Something wrong?" he questioned, wondering what could be so urgent.

"I own a brothel! There I've said it." Jess forgot all the words she had rehearsed since his letter arrived.

Sitting, startled by her confession, Sebastian was dumfounded. "You own a what?" he asked, thinking she was joking.

Seeing his face crumble and, between sobs, Jess tried to gather her thoughts, "It's not how it sounds," Jess began. "Julia and I are business partners for couples to meet and pair up." Taking a breath she added, "With the hope of a future together." A lie, hoping to pave the way for a full-blown confession.

"An agency?" he finally questioned, looking ashen.

"Sort of!" This was as hard as Julia said it would be.

"And you didn't think to explain this before we…?" He was beyond bewildered.

"We play no part in our customers' response to each other," she snatched a second breath. "Julia and I are front of house. No direct intervention, we have staff to organise everything. We add our financial elbow, that's all," she ended, searching his eyes for a reaction.

No matter how hard she tried to get the momentum back, this was a disaster. Dusting himself down, Sebastian turned to the car, "I think we should go."

"I had hoped to explain things better. I had no idea I would fall in love with you," Jess began the original script. "You see, I had a vision from the slums I could make a better life for myself without the help of others. It's been a long hard road to achieve financial security without succumbing to devious manipulative individuals. When you come from nothing, it's difficult to climb up, but I had high hopes and love didn't enter my head until I met you." Jess hesitated, thinking her words were exactly how it was. There was no need to make up scenarios. This was her life in a nutshell.

Sitting and looking over the view as the sun set, Sebastian took her hand. "I have no idea how I feel. You have explained and I understand your reasoning. I can't say if there is a way forward, as I'm still in shock. All I know is I love you desperately and have since the first moment we met." A tear in his eye, emotion overwhelming, he fell silent.

"I love you too and had hoped we would overcome the difficulties. I rehearsed many ways of explaining, but nothing can be said that unravels a life already lived." Jess sat shattered.

"Maybe if we take one day at a time?" Sebastian was trying hard to reconcile his passion with the inevitable fallout of such a confession.

"Skeletons in cupboards are hard to disguise when the door opens," Jess whispered honestly.

"Are there any others in your cupboard before we continue?" Sebastian asked, hoping not.

Although the death of Edward hung heavy on her conscience, Jess thought it better to leave it out for now. "I've had a colourful past, which may not defy scrutiny," Jess replied.

Holding the car door open, Sebastian shook his head trying to find a way through the quandary of true love versus respectability.

The journey onward was silent. Jess feared making things worse and Sebastian speechless with her revelations.

Never would two people try harder to find a solution to an age-old dilemma. Compatibility versus family values was a quagmire of contrasts which even the most competent strategists have no answer.

Their arrival at Jess's mansion saw Sebastian's jaw drop. His perception, pre-arrival, had been a back street terrace on a sleezy street. In his wildest dreams, he wouldn't have imagined a magnificent colonial mansion. He could have been forgiven for thinking, from the outside, this was the president's residence.

Jess said nothing as Sebastian stared out of the window to not only the spectacular building, but the vast estate that spread out before him as they drove along the tree lined driveway.

Desmond, awaiting their arrival, opened the door and greeted Jess as if royalty. "Welcome home, miss. I hope you've a had nice day. And Mr Sebastian, I presume?" he almost bowed.

"Yes, thank you, Desmond," Jess replied. "Sebastian, this is Desmond. Should you need anything, he will be happy to help," Jess introduced him with a smile, hoping to hide her despair.

"Pleased to meet you, sir!" Desmond held open the door.

"Likewise!" Sebastian replied, open-mouthed as he tried to take it all in.

As they entered the baronial hallway, Desmond carried Sebastian's case from the car. "Your room is on the second floor. Should you need anything, please call down. My number is on your dressing table." Desmond made his exit, nodding to the bellboy to take the guest's case to his room.

Shrugging his shoulder, Sebastian looked around. "You were kidding me, right?" he said, checking out the paintings along the staircase.

"Partly. The facilities may be different, but the business is the same," Jess tried to explain without elaborating.

Pondering her answer, he looked into her eyes. "By that I take it your clients are the rich and famous?"

"For the most part. Some are dignitaries, some leaders of large companies and some government officials. We also have one royal," Jess faltered, awaiting his reaction.

"A high-class brothel then?" You could hear a pin drop.

"When you put it like that…." Trying to hold back tears, Jess moved towards the bar. "I think I need a drink."

"Make mine a double," Sebastian replied, trying to reconcile the sordid with the ambience.

"A bit early for you?" Sandy the bouncer-cum-temporary barman smiled toward Jess, holding out a hand to Sebastian in a welcoming gesture.

"Sandy, this is my friend Sebastian," Jess said, using the word friend, not passionate lover. "Is Julia around?"

"She asked if you had arrived back. She is walking the dogs," he pointed to the palatial glass doors leading to the courtyard.

The sun was warm. The scent of the flowers and vegetation intoxicating, as Sebastian viewed an ancient garden fit for a queen.

He couldn't hold back an intake of breath as the full extent of Jess's fortune became obvious. Had this not been achieved by dubious means, he would have been in seventh heaven.

The moment the dogs spotted Jess, they began to run. Bending down, holding out her arms in welcome, they almost pushed her to the ground with excitement. Kneeling, rubbing of ears, licking, wagging, the love her dogs shared with Jess was obvious, "Hello, my lovely boys," Jess whispered as Sebastian's love for her overwhelmed him.

Despite his family's bias, he had to find a way to resolve the disparity of lifestyles. How he would achieve it was the burning question.

His mother was unhappy with his lifestyle and his father had a medieval approach to anything other than the rules he set out. He couldn't forget his siblings' attitude of superiority, born of a pampered upbringing and private schools. The more he considered his options, the more he hankered an orphan status.

It would be easy for him to fit in. He already had a need to distance himself from his privileged childhood. He travelled to parts of the world his parents had only read about and his up themselves brothers and sisters considered anything outside England behind the times. Hell would freeze over before any of them would accept Jess's chosen way of life.

Never having been swayed by his family's idea on how to behave or keeping the family standard above the parapet, perhaps he should say nothing, leaving them in the dark as to his whereabouts alongside Jess's social standing.

Everything he knew was on the table, except leaving Jess.

Chapter Twenty-One

The reunion between Julia and Sebastian was strained, not a warm and comfortable exchange between holiday acquaintances as hoped. How could there be with so many unspoken words and Jess's secrets laid bare?

The sun shining, a holiday romance shared by two people now a mire of entangled feelings, Julia felt desperately sad for them both.

Trying hard not to add to the dilemma, Julia held back from asking the obvious 'Is everything ok?', knowing there was no way to help a situation only Jess and Sebastian could resolve.

Sebastian had yet to encounter an evening when their clients arrived to sample the delights of the body in exchange for financial reward.

This was set to be a humongous challenge with the likes of Clinton, who considered it his right to outrageously flatter Jess for his own titillation, and the dignitaries who kept secrets from their wives, thinking it amusing to boast of their prowess between the sheets.

How Sebastian would reconcile his lifestyle as a photographer with hers and Jess's sordid agenda, Julia had no idea.

Trying to stall the inevitable, Jess suggested she and Sebastian eat out. The only issue? All the local 'culinary delight' restaurants were owned by her clients.

One nudge-nudge wink-wink and her resolve would crumble.

Settling for an out-of-town eating house at the risk of being disappointed, Jess booked a table at a bistro overlooking a lake.

"Why do I have a feeling you're stalling me being introduced to your clients?" his query loaded with innuendo.

"Is it so obvious? I had hoped you'd think I wanted to be alone with you," Jess lied, knowing stalling was her real intention.

"Jess, I may not have known you long, but I am a man of the world and know exactly what your business entails."

Sebastian's reply shocked her. "By that, do you mean you have partaken?" she asked, hoping not.

"I have no need," he laughed out loud at her suggestion. "I am a photographer, not a philanderer."

The now relaxed conversation and mutual affection began a night of reflection not of her business, but of the time they spent in St Lucia.

Taking his hand as they returned for a night of glorious intimacy, "This way!" Jess whispered, leading Sebastian through the kitchen and up the back stairs.

"I feel like a thief in the night!" Sebastian joked as they entered her luxurious suite. "On second thought, make that I've died and gone to heaven!" he smiled, drawing her into his arms, having seen the giant four-poster bed.

***

Days passed before Sebastian was allowed to join Jess in her role as 'madam'.

"The Queen of Tarts," he laughed, seeing Jess's reflection in the mirror. "I think the feathers in your hair are a little over the top." He grinned, "And the show of breasts should be for my eyes only." He patted her backside in a show of affection.

"No mixing with the ladies," Jess retorted. "You're mine and don't you forget it!" she threatened, checking her image once more. "I do look a little overdressed," she pondered, tempted to strip off for a night of passion as Sebastian gazed in the mirror with one hand on her breast.

"We better go now if we are to leave at all," Sebastian replied, reading her mind and snuggling her ear.

"Must we?" she grinned, hoping to be restrained.

A comic strip was how Julia explained the evening when next she met up with Jess. "You watch him and he watches you. Why don't you add a dog lead?" She laughed, having kept an eye on the pair.

"He seemed a little over-attentive to some of the girls. I was jealous," Jess complained.

Julia laughed, "From where I stood, all I could see was him puffing up red in the face each time you smiled at a client."

Summing up, Julia suggested a talk. "You need to reach an understanding if this is to work. This a business and you are its patron. Leave your romance behind and get on with the job." Adding, "Trust is the name of the game and without it, you may as well end it before it drives you both insane."

"You're right, of course, but that's easier said than done. My body says one thing, and my brain another. I've not experienced these feelings before. Ok, I've felt protective, but never this building anger."

"It's early days and you're in love. What did you expect?" Julia smiled.

"I'll speak to him!" Jess added, uncertain of the outcome.

Finishing the conversation with Julia, thinking how many feelings she harboured compared to the past, Jess wondered if she would ever be the same.

Fatigued with the ongoing saga of how he and his family would react, having discovered he reciprocated her love, now jealousy, anger and a passion that overwhelmed her entered the equation.

Why, she asked herself, *would anyone crave these emotions?* Before, it was straightforward. A man to provide for her financially and in bed. When that failed, building a business. Yes, it was stressful, but nothing like what she was experiencing now.

Finally, she understood Edward. This is not a game you can switch on and off. The overpowering emotions seemed to run your life and not the other way around.

If Sebastian felt only half, he would understand. If he didn't, she would sound like the women she once ridiculed. Deluded!

In a constant state of feeling the need for reassurance, panic when he spoke to other women, it was driving her mad.

Jess had a feeling women saw love differently, more emotionally. Men, on the other hand, were more bodily-driven.

Maybe the need to procreate was the answer, although, until now, having children hadn't entered Jess's mind.

Bodily perhaps did men a disservice, as some must have a strong sense of chemistry. It hadn't occurred to her before. In her business, many men stayed with their wives even when seeking out her floosies. Not forgetting the same applied the other way around, many of her ladies were married with children and their service was a practical solution to hardship.

With more questions than answers, Jess would never solve the testosterone versus hormone quandary.

"Sebastian, I need to explain something to you!" Jess looked under her eyes.

"Yes, my darling, explain away!"

Seeing his smile, this was not going to be easy! "I was thinking about men and women and how they react differently."

"To what?" Sebastian was fascinated.

"To love, stupid!"

Sebastian laughed. "You want to teach me the facts of life. A bit late for that, don't you think?" he laughed.

"No, of course not. My experience here has taught far more than your photography ever could."

"Oh! I don't know. Many naked women clients have taught me a lot about the female form," he continued to joke.

"Not what we look like, what we feel," Jess was struggling.

"Ahh, that's better. You want me to feel you?" he lunged towards her, taking her by surprise.

"Oh, please!" she said, exasperated that he had missed the point.

"I love it when you beg!" A deliberate play on words, Sebastian kissed her passionately and all thought of a serious conversation left her head.

The fur rug in front of the fire inspired her into a frenzy almost animal-like. "I'll show you what I mean," she shouted, leaving sucking bites almost everywhere.

Reciprocating, Sebastian retaliated, "I'll give you biting, my little viper," he grinned, holding her hands above her head, forcing his body into hers. "Now do you submit?" he looked deep into her eyes.

"Yes, yes, yes!" Jess uttered, feeling the rush of emotion she had sought to explain.

"Now, where were we? You wanted to explain something?" Sebastian smiled, having felt every emotion himself.

"I'm lost for words!" she replied. No words could possibly explain, she thought, wrapping her arms around his neck.

The saga of emotional highs followed by jealous lows continued to haunt her, "Perhaps marriage is the answer?" Jess asked of Julia.

"I'm not sure. You need to discover each other first," Julia advised.

"We've done more discovering than most people have in a lifetime." Jess grinned.

"Stop now. You know what I mean. The fabric of a successful marriage is based on far more than sex."

"And you know that how?" Jess replied, wondering where this lecture on human relationships was going, considering Julia had never been married.

Shaking her head, Julia did not want to divulge her own harrowing background. Despite her personal wealth, all had not run smoothly, not even with men. Although opposite to Jess's ambition of seeking men out, the outcome had been the same.

Wealth in abundance reaped its own problems. Some Julia had hidden so deep, it would be hard to discuss with anyone, even Jess.

"Sorry, Jess, I have someone waiting for me. We must talk later." Short but sweet, no intention of elaborating, Julia closed the door on the way out.

Chapter Twenty-Two

Good intentions always seemed to blight her efforts to discover someone to share her life with. Not the all-encompassing love Jess had finally found, someone to love and to be loved by, but in a less tormented way.

It seemed a lifetime now since her father suggested it was time for her to grow up and discover the delights of the world. "But finishing school?" Julia begged, not wanting to be sent away. "How will that teach me anything other than how to stand straight and speak with a plumb in my mouth?" Julia was adamant this was not for her.

Having packed her bag, the one person she thought would stand by her held out her passport and a flight ticket to the other side of the world. "But Mom, I don't want to leave you!" Having tried in vain, her mother had agreed it would be for the best.

"I thought you loved me?" All the pleading in the world counted for nothing. Her father had spoken and like a good wife, her mother had conceded that Julia's best chance of netting a suitable partner was to learn to behave like a lady. Whatever that meant? Julia remembered the conversation as if it were yesterday.

Returning suitably brain-washed, her persona was of the upper echelon. Following was a year without a soul she knew and didn't care to know. The finishing school was for spoilt brats whose fathers had inherited and not worked hard for their fortunes as Julia's had.

"Square peg, round hole," was how she explained the experience.

Her welcome home was hardly as she had expected. No longer the apple of her father's eye or the girl her mom had doted on, she felt left out of not only her parents' lives but also her so-called friends who shunned her for being 'posh'.

Julia, no idea where her place in the lives of her family or others was, began moving in circles made of her own fruition.

Mostly, this was easy with a generous allowance, an apartment in a fashionable part of town and a car to suit her image. "Go out and enjoy yourself," was her father's parting shot when he really meant, "Get from under our feet and do your own thing." And make no mistake, Julia did.

Attracting every hanger-on imaginable, Julia lived the high life. Nothing, it seemed, was too good or bad for the girl with a fortune and no boundaries. Julia could have been forgiven for thinking she was orphaned with the amount of time she spent living it up without constraint and no one to care where she was or what she did.

"Off the rails big style," was how her parole officer explained it to her parents, Julia having spent time in prison for violence on a march for 'Ban the Bomb'. "A closer eye on your sprog," were his words before writing out a list of dos and don'ts for her future welfare.

186

In her present mood, feeling neglected by her parents and shunned by her latest so-called friends, having been labelled a jailbird, Julia took herself in hand.

When the chips are down, the only way is up. Or so she thought until she met Simon. What happened next belied even her low expectations of humanity.

Sex was not the half of it. Drugs, all-night parties with the weird and wonderful of a time when flower power and music stimulated until exhausted, Julia, under Simon's influence, lived it all.

It was only when she woke to find Simon on top of her latest friend that the light turned on.

Unbelieving when he suggested she join them, followed by a string of expletives, Julia left her life of self-indulgence and made her way to the realtors.

With a stunning house over-looking the sea, Julia began life again. This time, no care for her parents' interference or a male to share with, she set to work on an investment program that turned her life around.

Having discovered an eye for property to be renovated and sold on, her name became renowned.

It was as if a gift had been bestowed upon her as her talents reaped more than her wildest dreams. It was not just the dollars that rolled in, but her business acumen and lifestyle that Julia was revered for throughout the property development world.

Going from strength to strength, Julia was the envy of her contemporaries. Women applauded the woman not interested in their men and, likewise, the male population drew inspiration from her talent for recognising a good investment.

Her portfolio swelled alongside her bank balance and popularity, with her presence sought after at events thought worthy.

No longer partaking of the fruits of the day, more a mingling of souls craving her latest venture, was how Julia explained her latest mantra. Giving nothing away until the deal was done, Julia rose to greater heights than even she thought possible.

Her office ran like clockwork, by females doing her bidding and males to discuss in which architectural wonder she should next invest her considerable wealth. No expense spared, Julia bought, restored, and sold once-dilapidated properties with exuberance.

No need for flattery or sex, the excitement of the end game in business was all she craved. As her bank overflowed with dollars, even the draw of independence she once harboured ceased to enthuse. It was time for Julia to seek a new venture.

This is when her direction changed again. Although her life was good when she first encountered Jess, it went from strength to strength. Soulmates was how she explained their newfound friendship. Not of the sort where men screwed up their lives with demands and an exuberance to spend their money, but a true friendship where likeminded people came together, not only for financial benefits, but the satisfaction of knowing they'd made it on their own.

Having experienced more upheaval than most, Jess and Julia settled into a shared project and 'J&J's Refined Escort Emporium' was born.

Following their original choice subject being thwarted, they took up the gauntlet with vigour, discovering an opportunity to satisfy not only their once wayward nature but that of their eager client base.

Sex for sale with style and elegance to overshadow royalty, their future looked rosy. Notwithstanding certain complications, their friendship was unwavering until now.

This latest turn of events, Sebastian with his draw to Jess and likewise hers to him, Julia worried. Recognising the difference between the sex and the shallow emotion Jess had shared with Mark, it seemed she was attached to Sebastian forever.

Maybe her lifestyle would deter him. If not, his family may intervene. Julia hoped so. Far be it from not wanting Jess to be happy. The torment inflicted so far by their choice of business and Jess's determination to keep him close threatened not only their friendship but the hard-won partnership she and Jess shared.

A strange ask she knew to keep the status quo, but, nevertheless, her own ambition had changed immeasurably since meeting up with Jess. No longer seeking a man with all their disparities, a less tormented lifestyle was now Julia's preference and she had hoped, long term, Jess felt the same.

Julia's need for a loving family had long since been snatched away. Maybe that and the antics of the men she attracted were the reasons she shied away from the norm.

Not wishing to study the rationale more deeply, Julia was tempted to help Sebastian on his way.

A word here and there, how would he know she wished rid of him and the threat she felt he posed. The last thing Julia wanted was to spoil things for Jess, but Sebastian, she felt, had entered the stage with his own agenda. Not destroying their business or the stability of it for the future but coming between her and her friend after all they had been through would be a bitter pill to swallow.

Julia had seen it many times. One partner dedicated to business, the other torn between a family life and keeping pace. It was on the cards for a separation and Julia had no taste for it.

Although unexpected, the letter from her mom was a comfort.

"Dearest Julia,

We have missed you so. Please contact us as your father has not been well for some time.

Love, Mom."

Short but sweet. It wasn't until Julia read between the lines that it occurred to her this was not a letter of reconciliation.

Why? Julia asked herself, after all this time of not caring where or what she was up to, did her mom feel compelled to write.

The morning papers answered the question:

"Fall from grace. Entrepreneur gambles his fortune on a failing company deal...."

"Hi Mom,

Sorry, but I'm busy right now. My business has taken off big style and I can't get away but thank you for thinking of me."

Julia remembered her mom's harsh words as she waved her goodbye (it's for the best) even now.

No need to ask how her father was. It was obvious. Not an illness as such, but the weight of his wallet now a feather and his bank account empty. It took all of Julia's restraint not to laugh.

It had been years since she left her family home to mix with people she thought more in tune with her life. Julia was now sober (well almost). No drugs or sex and she had built a business with Jess, supposedly as a pillar of the society her mom and dad had hoped she would adopt.

Not exactly their standard! Julia mused, she could almost hear her parents scream. "A brothel? My God! Have you gone mad?" Julia laughed. If only they knew!

Chapter Twenty-Three

At four o-clock in the morning, there was a knock on the bedroom door. Looking through the peephole, Jess checked her watch. "What time do you think this is?" annoyed, she opened the door with the strength of a body builder.

Chris looked shocked with the stern look on her face, "Sorry Jess, I needed to speak to you yesterday, but you were, 'Hmm!' otherwise engaged." He took a step back.

Not taking in his words, she looked to see if Sebastian had woken. "What can be so urgent you have to wake me at this hour?" she murmured quietly, seeing Sebastian turn over.

"I thought you should see this. It was hand-delivered late last night." He passed Jess an envelope with an official-looking crest.

Completely awake, she slit open the letter and began to read…. "My God, we have an inspection by the business regulators. Go explain to the girls they have the day off, pay them the going rate and tell them not to return until late. Then, wake Julia and ask her to meet me in the breakfast room." Turning, she took a breath. "Did any of the men pay for the night?" Jess added, frantic not to be seen running a brothel.

"I don't think so. It's usually on weekends!"

"Good. Check anyway!" She knew that sometimes they broke the rules. "Also, ask Howard to check the grounds. I don't want any strays left over from last night walking around." Jess tried to think of everything.

She dressed in haste. Sebastian was still asleep and had no idea what was going on. Taking the stairs two at a time, Jess met Julia in the hallway.

"Why so late to deliver the mail?" Julia asked, lifting a gent's hat from the coat stand. "What time do the inspectors arrive?" she looked around the dining hall still regaled in last night's frivolities.

"Maybe it's a tip-off and they're trying to catch us out!" Jess read aloud the lines she failed to read earlier. "12.30 this afternoon. My God, we only have this morning to straighten things out."

Jess sighed, picking up the phone, "Can you ask your people to come over right away? As many as you can. We have a twelve-o-clock meeting with the council here today," she asked her client and owner of the cleaning agency.

Julia didn't hear the answer, but from the look on Jess's face, she knew they would arrive soon.

Chris looked jaded. "The girls will be out of here as soon as they are dressed. Any men left over have been instructed to make a quiet exit. Sandy will drive home the ones expecting a taxi. Everyone will be out by at least nine o-clock." He took a breath.

"We have the cleaners arriving within the hour and Julia and I will do a final check. Let me know when

Howard is finished in the garden. We will take the dogs for a short walk just before they arrive, giving the impression we are relaxed with their visit," Jess looked up just as Sebastian came down the stairs.

"Morning, sweetheart, you're up early," he smiled, kissing her cheek.

"I hope you don't mind, darling, but I've arranged for you to ride to the village this morning with Chris. The horses need a workout, so I thought it would be a good opportunity for you to meet the villagers," Jess adlibbed.

"It's a beautiful morning. I can't think of anything better. Are you going to join us?" Sebastian asked, an arm around her waist.

Jess kissed him gently, "Sorry, next time. I have some catching up with Julia. Some boring figures to go over. Why don't you lunch at the pub? Chris deserves a treat. He's been working hard lately."

"If that's ok with you?" Sebastian turned to Chris.

Smiling as if he had nothing better to do, Chris said, "It will be a pleasure. See you at the stables at eleven thirty." His acting abilities smiled upon by both Jess and Julia, Chris winked as he walked away.

The frantic next few hours as they ushered the girls and left over clients into cars, limousines, and taxis was described as a fire prevention inspection.

They apologized to the rich and famous for the inconvenience, promising them a free evening's entertainment on their next visit. "Were sorry to give you such short notice, but you know how busy the fire departments are. No time to stand on ceremony."

"Best to be safe!" The chief fire officer agreed, wondering why he had no knowledge of the inspection.

Thinking on her feet, Jess added, "Insurance. What would we do without it?" Her smile and outstretched hand reassured him it was genuine.

The cleaners suitably warned to get the job done by twelve o-clock sharp, Julia and Jess searched the rooms making sure no stragglers were still wandering around.

Howard, having found only one perfectly suited and booted individual stretched out under a wisteria-covered pagoda, helped him to his feet. "This way, sir. Time for home," he instructed, having notified Sandy to stand by.

"It's like a military operation," Julia said, watching the various teams finishing their duties.

Happy nothing had been missed and with congratulations all round, one after another of the workers filed past. In vans, cars and young gardeners on bikes, Julia and Jess waved as the last one closed the gates on their way out.

With just time to dress and look suitably relaxed, the pair sauntered across the lawns. The dogs were playing and running round. A typical lunchtime stroll was enacted.

Grinning, Jess looked toward Julia. "A bonus for everyone," she confirmed, as a party of six, three women and three men from the government, awaited their pleasure on the terrace.

"Good afternoon, I'm Jessica and this is Julia. So pleased you could join us. Lemonade, anyone?" Jess smiled, an outstretched hand indicating the comfortable garden furniture.

On cue, the maid arrived with an ice bucket and freshly squeezed lemonade.

The idyllic surroundings admired, "Now, where shall we begin?" a more austere member of the team asked, looking every bit like a sergeant major.

"Would you care to visit our school room?" Jess should have said, 'Our hastily pulled together anti-room filled with desks and chairs from the storeroom.'

"Why not? I take it you have lectures on social behaviour?" their client and friend asked, a wink towards Julia out of sight of his team.

"Indeed, we do. But, as requested, only a selection of students have been asked to attend your visit today. Normally, the sessions are full."

Sally, Freida, Susan, and Marjory had been selected from their list of girls. Dressed appropriately for the inspection and versed in what to say and do. "Keep your mouths shut and smile politely. I will prompt you when to answer their questions," Julia had instructed and, although the tone was stilted, Susan, chosen as the most educated, acted her part beautifully.

"The gardens play a vital role in their education," Jess began. "Knowing the types of flowers and shrubs is

196

always an asset when attending their 'coming out'. Most men of respectability appreciate their wives having knowledge of how to recognise flora and fauna. We have different breeds of horses in our private stables. Dogs home trained and many wild species for them to identify." Speaking as if a fountain of knowledge, Jess smiled.

Julia came in without a break for silence, "We have a library with books from many ancient and modern 'Masters of Literature'. Lecturers are invited frequently to answer questions on any subject the girls have found difficult understanding. And, of course, Jess and I are educated in many subjects they may find interesting."

"Without a doubt!" Jess whispered to Julia, whilst smiling sweetly toward the appreciating inspectors.

"For their suitors, most men are advised to take their time in deciding which partner would suit them best. It is proven 'marry in haste, repent at leisure', is the mantra for an unhappy union."

Much nodding and smiling, the three women agreed. The men on the team thinking from a man's point of view, this may prove more problematic. "In certain cases where men need a wife to take part in their business activities, sooner rather than later may be better." The male team mouthpiece suggested.

Jess and Julia nodded their agreement. "Sexist fool," Julia whispered to Jess as the pair nodded once more.

Having feasted on fresh salmon from their saltwater farm and tea specially selected from India, the quorum began a tour led by Jess of the various rooms of interest. Leaving out their bordello bathtubs made for two, four-poster beds draped in lace and mirrored ceiling to titillate the clients, the team of inspectors smiled their approval.

All in all, it was a great success. Handing the signed certificate of excellence for J&J's Refined Escort Emporium for the next twelve months, the councillor general with a smile and a wink, whispered behind his hand, "See you later, Jess!" before ushering his party down the steps to the waiting limousines.

Waving as they drove away, Julia, pleased to see the back of them, sighed a sigh of relief.

"Yes!" Jess punched the air, realising all their hard work had been a success.

"I think you pair would have convinced them with or without old dirty Harry," Chris laughed, pouring the last of the champagne into crystal goblets.

"I'll drink to that!" Jess added.

Unable to contain herself, Julia laughed, "If you mean the Right Honourable Harold Withstanding, I'm sure if he heard your description, we would have been demoted to sleezy hovel."

Chapter Twenty-Four

A period of settled happiness rested over the mansion. Nothing had been heard of Edward's relatives, obviously resigned to his wayward past. Sandy, reconciled with the horror of the night he died, concentrated once more on his new duties. Following his promotion, these included not only head of chauffeurs and welcoming clients, but also the stables and organising horse riding sessions.

Howard was satisfied the restoration and position of the conservatory was a roaring success. With his headship over the café and the now fourteen-strong fully-trained gardeners, he concentrated more on client guidance around the arboretum and making sure no one overstayed their welcome.

Josie, promoted to house mother, looked after her girls' well-being, wardrobes and keeping them safe from possible abusers. Alongside this, any difficulties with parenting were now her soul responsibility. Working tirelessly, Josie's esteem grew with her pay packet.

Chris, in his capacity of managing director, took charge of everything and everyone, including his staff of many. His promotion had been the best decision yet made by Jess and Julia, giving them more time to spend on life.

Jess's life with the help of Sebastian had gone from strength to strength. No more cat and mouse games, it was considered the optimum of relationships. Even Julia wondered why she'd worried.

Julia was the only enigma. No one, even Jess, could work it out. Casual friends, yes, but any meaningful relationships were kept at bay and, when questioned, she withdrew into a dark place. A pretend smile, a hearty shrug and the next one was dismissed to the rank and file.

Jess worried for Julia's future. There are lonely years ahead if you're on your own, especially when you're older. She would always have Jess, but even that was uncertain.

Sebastian wanted more of her attention and the mention of a family was constantly up there with her meeting his parents. Alongside holidays to the Caribbean where his heart lay before meeting her. How Julia would fare if the business was sold, she had no idea.

"I'm in it for the long haul," Julia boasted, hoping Jess felt the same.

Had Jess not met Sebastian, maybe she would have agreed, but her life had changed for the better now and she had no intention of losing the chance of a happy ever after.

"My love for you will last forever," Jess whispered sentiments from the heart. His reply took Jess to another level.

His body in hers was all she craved as he replied, "I love you so. I had no idea of life's meaning until I met you."

No matter the draw of Julia and the business, their close bond grew. Jess was hooked on the love she had found and felt sure Sebastian felt the same. 'Lifetime partners' was how Jess explained to Julia as she displayed his ring.

Their marriage was set for early spring of the following year. The mansion was to be transformed from debauchery to heavenly with the aid of many wedding planners.

A sparkling new pearlescent cream limousine stood outside as their girls stood in admiration.

The ribbons and flowers were demonstrated to Jess for the big day. "It will be a wonderland," Jess twirled around in front of the mirror as Julia looked on, a tear in her eye.

"You look stunning," Julia murmured, afraid this was the beginning of the end for their dream.

Although not wanting to pre-empt her reply, Julia felt obliged to ask, "What of our business when you are a married woman?" trying to keep the conversation light.

"What do you mean? I have no intention of leaving the business unless you want me to?" Jess looked crestfallen, never having given the idea a second thought.

"I just wondered. You may want children and this is no place to bring them up."

Stopping in her tracks, Jess had no idea how to reply. So wrapped up in her wonderland of expectations of a life with Sebastian, procreation only passed her mind once before. Jess had no idea how to reply.

Removing her wedding gown, carefully laying it on the bed, "I will let you know," Jess replied, a tear in her eye, thinking Julia wouldn't want her once she was married.

"Sebastian," Jess cried, "Julia won't want me when we wed. I think the idea of having children around is the reason!"

Gulping air before answering, Sebastian had long thought through what would happen if Jess got pregnant. "I'm sure that's not the case. She loves you like a sister. Maybe she is thinking of our children and how they would fit in." He was about to say, "in a brothel", but thought better of it as Jess looked ready to cry.

Unable to answer, Jess sat on the bed. All she had thought before was how wonderful it would be running in the garden with the dogs and sharing special moments with Julia, Sebastian, and their children.

It was a monumental shock to think she would have to leave her precious home with all she'd put into it. The realisation she may have to give it up stunned her like nothing before.

Chris, his professional head on, suggested a meeting. "We can discuss the way forward with everyone present. Whatever the decision, it will affect us all."

"Maybe so," Jess finally agreed, having thought through the possibilities.

Julia, realising Jess had withdrawn from her, was devastated. In her wildest dreams, the end of their friendship and business was the last thing she wanted.

Spending hours deliberating, Jess thought of everything but failed to see a way forward.

Chris, Howard, and Sandy had their heads together well before decision day. "I've got it!" Chris shouted and began writing each detail for and against down in readiness for 'doomsday', as Jess suggested the day would be.

Chris consulted everyone he could think of to make his plan work. Forget the hierarchy clients, he had them by the balls.

No one would complain. How could they? Being regulars had sealed their vote. The final decision was down to Jess, Julia, and Sebastian to discover a way through the melee that had been raging for days.

"A proper little up-himself director," Sebastian smiled as Chris banged the gavel.

"Ladies and gentlemen, I call to order this meeting to discuss the future of our employment. Of all of us!" he looked around the room.

"The situation to be discussed is due to the nature of the issue in hand. The marriage of Jess to Sebastian."

Chris stood to attention, the gavel raised, as Julia interrupted, "Yes, yes, we all know the reason for the meeting. What we need to know is the solution if there is one?"

"With respect, I'm coming to that. We have spent hours going over the pros and cons." What he really meant was he had spent a day and night going over the possibilities, not only of his plan, but contacts to be obtained from everyone needed to carry it through.

Handing out files to each person around the table, Julia and Jess decided to let him have his say. "Get on with it then. We have all spent time seeking out a solution," Jess said, feeling drained that it had come to this before she and Sebastian could marry.

"You will see my plan is a long-term solution, covering most of the issues raised. Page one…" The team dutifully opened the files with much shuffling and muttering before he continued.

"You can see an architect's plan marking out how many acres the project would take away from the current mansion."

Before Chris could continue, Sebastian was the first to speak, "You did all this yourself?" he questioned, as the others looked on in amazement.

"Not exactly. I've had many meetings with people more qualified than me. The idea was mine, but without the professionals, I was unsure how we could make it work."

"It's perfect," Jess jumped from her seat, throwing her arms around his neck.

"You see, we could plant trees around the area to the right of the property and at the rear, cars could join the existing driveway."

Before he could continue, Julia joined in the hug, "You are a wonder. What would we do without you?" Tears were streaming down her face as the solution stared them in the face.

"Congratulations," Sebastian shook his hand.

"I always knew you could do it!" Howard and others joined in.

Jess, now her professional head on, having studied the detail, "I take it you have our team of builders standing by?"

"Just the signatures of our council registrar and planning regulator and we're good to go. We can be sure of their support," he added with a grin, knowing they were party to the pleasures of the brothel.

Howard stood, looking on, "Is it possible to keep the walled garden? It's a favourite with the clients."

"The planners have instructed how much would be needed to separate the two properties. The sheep will need to be moved closer to J&J's but other than that, there are plenty of acres left."

"What about funding?" Sebastian gingerly asked, wondering how he would fund even a small section of the plan.

Chris turned the pages, "This is the section that sets out the cost. It's not cheap, as you can see, but I feel sure it will be worthwhile." He handed each one a copy of the breakdown. "We have many that can assist. It may need J&J to close for a short time. Maybe we could call it a holiday break while the boundaries are established and planted out?"

"My men can help with that!" Howard suggested with pride.

"All in favour, raise a hand." Chris said, gavel raised once more, was confident this was it!

Chapter Twenty-Five

A mini mansion would be perfect. Not just for separation from the brothel, but when Sebastian's family arrived to scrutinise their son's fiancée, they would see a spacious countryside home fit for any member of his family.

The cost would only dent Jess's fortune and she wondered why they hadn't thought of it before. A perfect solution to many difficult issues.

Julia would remain in the big mansion to oversee the business with Jess involved as and when. Although the building remained in Jess's name, the restoration and setup cost had been funded by Julia and wouldn't have happened without her. Their lawyers had drawn up a totally agreed upon contract for every event, so all was good.

The problem as far as Jess and Sebastian were concerned was that their wedding had to be postponed. It would take time to complete the build and for his family to have a place to stay away from the brothel. This also meant the reception would have to be scaled down and arranged in a more modest setting.

"Throw as much money as is needed to get the job done. Not shoddy, you understand. I want the same experts who restored the brothel to carry out the work," Jess instructed Chris who, as usual, was on the case.

"No problem, Jess. I have already scheduled their time to begin right away." Chris smiled. Once he had thought up the scheme and confirmed all the legals and plans, he had paid a deposit himself to hold the builders' time.

Realising the value of someone of Chris's ingenuity, Jess suggested he be offered shares in the business. "Not instead of his salary," which had increased substantially since he began, "but on top?" Jess said and Julia welcomed the idea.

"He's worth his weight in gold," Julia replied. "I can't tell you how happy I am with the solution." The girls hugged, another weight off their minds.

The struggles of the past and recently seemed to melt away in the euphoria of organising the interior design of her new home, "Don't you think it a little premature?" Sebastian, never having to concern himself with such things before, commented, seeing Jess through the mirror as he shaved.

"Your part in the project will be to take pictures for the record when it's finished. Not forgetting the nursery!" Jess ignored his comments and continued to check materials and colour cards.

Sebastian's eyes lit up. "Can we practice now?" he turned towards her. Half-shaved, half not, but fully naked, his ardour was obvious.

As he removed her negligée, Jess took his manhood in her hand and sighed, "Practice makes perfect, so they tell me!" A temptress smile lured him to the four-poster.

It was midday before they finally came down for breakfast. "You mean brunch, do you not?" Chris smiled, removing breadcrumbs from the table with a napkin. "Late-night, was it?" he grinned, placing fruit and yogurt on the table instead of eggs benedict on pancakes with syrup.

"Sarcasm is the lowest form of wit," Sebastian laughed. "Just coffee for me."

"I'm starving," Jess looked Sebastian in the eye.

"Give me a break, woman," he replied as her toes reached his crotch under the table.

This time, the building machinery and many boots took the back road. Hedgerows between the big mansion and the new one were planted by Howard's men. Soil removed by the ton for the footings, it seemed to be happening all at once.

Proud overseer Sebastian took photographs and made sketches at each milestone as work began on the most important event in his life, other than marrying Jess, of course!

Not having been aware of his talent as an artist, Jess requested he paint a canvas of the mansion for the staircase. "I will also paint a portrait of you in your finery, my darling," he added, a picture of her reflection in the mirror crossing his mind.

Under the watchful eye of John, the master builder who had headed the first restoration, studying the plan as heavy good vehicles arrived carrying stone and seasoned timber to match the big mansion, everything was carefully thought through and would be built with precision under his scrutiny.

Every spare moment, Jess and Julia visited the site. Machinery the likes of which they only vaguely remembered, it was hard to imagine the result amongst the multiple activities.

The build was guided by their project manager, Terry McIntyre, and many top bricklayers and agile labourers. The progress was remarkable.

One of the most important facets to the project was the wall dividing the two mansions, which was to be as high as possible. The instructions were clear. One door led to the big mansion, security coded and locked with only two master keys, one for Jess and the other for Julia.

Only a select few were given the code and trusted to keep their secret. It was to be disguised by foliage and never used during Sebastian's family visits.

Fort Knox was how the locksmith explained it. "No one's getting through this sucker," the guy, given carte blanche, assured, demonstrating his masterpiece of locks used by banks and most financial institutions.

Jess and Sebastian's residence was to be their haven. Strictly protected from prying eyes, anyone breaking the rules was under threat of dismissal at least. At most, should they disobey, "Well, who knows?" Jess grinned.

Although satisfied with the status quo, Sebastian was aware his contribution was superficial, with no monetary assistance. At best, his artistic skills would receive only smiles of appreciation and at worst, no one would notice.

Not wishing to be a kept man long term, his suggestion he rent a studio uptown to pursue his career, which prior to his arrival in America was extremely lucrative, didn't meet the response expected.

"You want to work in town?" Jess's surprise was unforeseen.

"I'm no gigolo. I would like to help keep my family!" he said, smiling, lifting Jess into the air, thinking she would be happy with the idea.

"There's no need for you to work. The business reaps far more than we could spend in a lifetime," she replied to Sebastian's chagrin.

Looking deep into her eyes, he whispered, "Jess, I have my own ambition for our future. Our children, our home, and our equal status are important to me. A studio in town would be a perfect solution, passing trade until I have built a reputation and somewhere to hold my exhibitions." He was downcast that she should think him satisfied to stay by her side without ambition.

Jess stood looking through the window overlooking the garden. Her thoughts returned to her previous romantic encounters, where, after a while, the relationships broke down. "We could add a studio and a place for you to exhibit your work in the house and invite clients…." Sebastian was shaking his head.

"For taking 'bread and butter' pictures such as travel documents, I would need passing foot fall. For family portraits likewise and, for fashion shoots, I would be away from home anyway. I'll be back each night as most businesspeople are.

"I may find the need to travel sometimes. Maybe we could combine my overseas contracts with a holiday?" He was trying hard to persuade Jess, who had hoped he would form a team alongside her and Julia.

"It just seems…." Jess hesitated as his arm came around her. A finger to her lips, Sebastian gently kissed her.

"I'm not leaving you. I love you. I have ambitions that I need to satisfy. It will make us stronger." He held her tight.

"I know but..." Once more he kissed her, this time more passionately.

"Don't, Jess. Without a life of my own, I would be stifled. That doesn't mean I don't love you, you know I do!"

Had they been in bed and not strolling the garden with the dogs, he would have proved it.

"Hi!" the sound of Julia interrupted. "We need a strong arm!" she smiled, taking Sebastian's arm, not seeing the look on Jess's face. "I'll have him back in no time," she laughed, guiding him to the patio where Chris and Sandy were trying to move a stone statue.

Sitting pensive, Jess mulled over her past experiences, thinking every man she had known had had their own agenda. None the same as Sebastian's, as she could see some merit in his suggestion, but nevertheless, all her other relationships had ended the same.

"Maybe this time," she muttered to her dogs, "it will be different?" Wagging and jumping, Diesel and Jeremy temporarily took her attention away from her harrowing thoughts.

Seeing Sebastian, the dogs ran at full speed. Jess, seeing him approach, his tall strong body and handsome face, she melted. He was the love of her life and this time, she would let nothing stand in the way.

"Over here, darling!" he beckoned. "What do you think?" hand pointing to the statue's new position.

If only he knew what she was thinking, the statue would fade into insignificance compared to what she had in mind for this man she adored. "Coming!" Jess shouted, waving her agreement. *Nothing,* Jess thought, *will separate me from Sebastian, the love of my life.*

Taking him in her arms, the dogs going wild with affection as she and Sebastian embraced, her whispered words of passion saw their disappearance to the privacy of the bedroom.

Her need was so great, that Jess thought she would burst with the inner turmoil of her emotions. Unable to control her primeval instincts, she ripped open his shirt, unzipped his trousers and pushed him to the bed.

No need for words, his body responded. Sebastian, likewise, undressed Jess, kissing her all over with fervour. He knew for certain this woman, no matter the difficulties, would remain by his side and in his bed forever.

Their lovemaking was more intense than ever before. They had made love many times, but this was different. It was as if life itself depended upon their every move.

Never before had they indulged each other in ways that defied reason. Sebastian, out of control for the first time in his life, his excitement reaching a climax, timed perfectly as Jess's nails pierced, signalling her euphoria.

"My God, what was that?" Sebastian, prostrate, lay drained.

Jess, lost for words, grinned. Running a finger from his neck to his nether region spoke volumes.

Chapter Twenty-Six

"Pregnant. You must be kidding?" checking the result from the clinic again, Julia confirmed there was no mistake.

Remembering, Jess knew the exact moment. "The house isn't finished!" was all she could manage, not considering the third finger of her left hand was vacant of a ring, or the consequences of running a very busy business. "What will he say?" Jess questioned. Once again, the timing would change her life forever.

"One risk taken, one problem to be solved," Julia's pontification did nothing to calm the waters.

Fate had dealt another card to be turned. How this one would be dealt with was anyone's guess. A wedding put off, a mansion only half built, Sebastian's family awaiting their son's invitation to a now 'shotgun wedding'. How he would explain their premarital sex to his up themselves parents and siblings, so proper that whiter-than-white wouldn't cut it, Jess had no idea. This was a disaster up there with Hiroshima.

Instead of ecstatic, as Jess's reaction should have been had this miraculous conception been later rather than sooner, everything would be fine. Well, not fine exactly, time off from the business to give birth, changing soiled nappies and no sleep from a baby screaming all night instead of entertaining the clients in gowns that fit perfectly. Jess looked in the mirror, tears running down her cheeks.

Throwing up was only one physical change that awaited. Lethargy from being fat, swollen ankles and breasts out of control, she had no idea how she would carry on.

Julia had a slightly different prospective, "It will be wonderful, Jess. Just think, a mirror image of Sebastian or a beautiful baby girl with hair the colour of fire just like yours. What more could you ask?"

It hadn't occurred to Jess until then that their baby may turn out to look like them. "Stop now," Jess replied. "I'm happy the way I am. Maybe in a few years, but now is definitely not the right time."

Julia looked shocked. "You mean you're not happy?"

"Happy? I'm devastated. I love my life as it is. This will change everything!" Thinking back how her mother and father had turned their backs on her and couldn't wait to off-load her made the whole experience worse.

She made Julia promise not to say a word to anyone, not even Sebastian. It was time to work out a plan. It would have to be quick, as a growing waistline may be disguised from the clients, but from Sebastian, impossible!

"What's up?" Her outward appearance was only part of the problem. Feeling sick and unable to eat, only two of the many occasions needed to be disguised from Sebastian.

Worst of all, her passion between the sheets was waning. Not from the physical attachment to Sebastian, but her 'hormones going wild'. Julia explained the phenomenon as a side effect playing havoc with her once animal-like nature.

"I'm scared he'll go off me!" Jess cried allowed, feeling unable to return his advances.

Not sure how to advise her, Julia took her hand, "You must explain. It will be best for both of you!"

"How will explaining I'm turning into a hippo with the sex drive of a nun help?" tears streaming, Jess wanted to crawl into a hole and die.

Scared for her friend's stability due to hormones, Julia tried another idea. "Pull yourself together, you're not dying. It's perfectly natural to be afraid, but women do this all the time." Julia sharpened her tone.

"Well, they can do it, but I'm not ready!" Jess retorted. This was not going well, Julia thought to herself, placing an arm around her shoulder.

The next few days saw Jess regress into herself. "Please, Jess, what have I done?" Sebastian asked, beside himself with worry.

"Nothing!" Sharp, Jess moved away from his advances.

"It must be something. I love you and want to show it," he said as Jess burst into tears. "Have I done something? Please tell me. I didn't mean it whatever it was!" His eyes looked sad.

"I'm pregnant. There, I've said it!" Jess shouted as Sebastian looked amazed.

"Is that all? That's wonderful, darling," he took her in his arms.

"For you, maybe. I'm the one having to suffer," Jess retorted to the shock of Sebastian.

"Suffer? What do you mean? It's the best thing that's happened!" He really had no idea Jess would react in this way.

"My life is over, just like my mom's. I'll be nothing more than a machine at its beck and call day and night." Jess sobbed.

"Whoa! Where did this come from?" Sebastian asked, bewildered by her reaction. "This is what our love is all about!" he tried to console her.

"How can you say that? Our relationship will go downhill and you will get another woman and…." Jess was distraught.

Suddenly realising he had no idea of her background, Sebastian took her hand, "Jess, I'm not your father. I love you more than words can say and our baby will make my life complete." He held her face between his hands and kissed her gently.

"But, but…." Sebastian kissed her mouth, preventing her from speaking.

"No buts. We'll work out the practicalities together. I don't care what people say or if the house isn't finished and, least of all, what our parents think. You and our baby are my priority from now on. We'll work through this, Jess. I promise." His warm smile and him holding her tight melted all the fears she had imagined.

Clinging as if life itself depended on it, Jess calmed down, "What about your family?" she insisted once more.

"They are the least of our worries. I'll speak to them tonight!"

"Please don't tell them I'm pregnant," Jess almost begged him.

"Ok, if you insist! I'll tell them I've won a painting contract in Haiti and will be away for a year. They won't question it, as it's normal for me." He grinned, "Let's not talk about them. I would like a little girl that looks like you!" He once again took Jess by surprise.

"No boy to carry on your blood line?" Jess smiled, the first time since reading the result.

***

The sixties were not the best time to have a baby out of wedlock, so Jess chose to disguise the event as long as possible. A brothel was no place to stop the comments. "Hi Jess, eaten the pillow, I see?" The first to get a two-finger gesture, Tom, a hotel owner and well-known client, laughed out loud.

Anyone asking why her bustle was on back to front would be subject to an instant kick up the backside. Well, ankle, as raising her leg higher would be impossible.

Running from the blackjack table to throw up, Jess saw eyebrows raised, but now no one dared say a word.

Time passed and their mansion was coming along splendidly. More builders than the Great Wall of China, treble the labourers, painters, decorators and interior designers by the dozen, the Palace of Versailles hadn't hosted more.

"Do you really think it will be ready for the day?" Jess asked as the gardeners walked over each other in haste to meet the deadline.

"Sure!" Howard confirmed, pointing to the flower beds. "Just the playground to be sorted and we're almost there." He smiled, seeing Jess struggle to get into the car.

Not the best day in her life, the birth came quick and fast as Sebastian tried to remember everything Jess needed for the hospital.

Expecting continuity, she was surprised to discover the contractions stopped. "Nothing to worry about," the sister assured her. "It's quite normal."

Nothing about this experience was normal. Breathing as if in a wind tunnel, unable to breathe out before a second intake of breath sent her head spinning with another body-paralyzing pain she had no control over.

"Pant," the instructions came fast and furious as the agony grew with every, "It's almost there!" A statement heard too many times for Jess's liking.

"I can't," was Jess's answer to the command 'bear down'. "More gas and air," was her reply.

The next moment, the sister screamed another impossible to obey instruction, "Come on, Jess, I can see its head!" These were the last words she heard just as an excruciating pain pushed her baby into the world.

"Congratulations, Jess, you have a beautiful baby girl." The words drifted as a bundle of warm wet baby was placed to her breast.

"Thank God!" Jess exclaimed, looking down as two brown unseeing eyes stared up. Tears streamed as the wonders of motherhood struck like a blow to her heart. Never in her wildest dreams did she think a feeling of complete love would be the result of such pain.

As if by magic, the last hours drifted from her memory, replaced by a feeling of unbelievable contentment as Jess cradled her miracle.

A silent stream of her trusted staff filed past the window as Sebastian, chest puffed up with pride, offered up his little girl for inspection. "Well, what do you think?" he murmured as Chris looked on, bewitched.

"She's, er, um, beautiful," he replied, seeing a pink and crinkly face under silky brown hair just visible above the blanket.

"Isn't she just?" Sebastian, displaying all the symptoms of a lovesick parent, gently rocked Pricilla Jane without removing his stare.

Julia was busy arranging bouquets in several vases. Jess's room was filling up with the most wonderful flowers money could buy. Friends, staff, clients, all enthralled by the birth, cared nothing for the protocol of 'cart before the horse'.

"Only your parents and siblings to tell and we're home and dry." Jess smiled, thinking their child would be one year old before the wedding was announced.

"Maybe Julia could pretend Pricilla Jane was hers for the day!" Sebastian smiled, "Julia!" he called out, "How do you fancy a virgin birth?" The three laughed.

"Not for a one-year-old!" she grimaced, taking hold of her soon-to-be goddaughter.

Chapter Twenty-Seven

The early seventies saw the end of the project. A party to end all parties was arranged for just a few. The less the clients knew, the less chance Jess and Sebastian's hideaway would be in the public domain.

A 'business venture' was how they explained the downsizing of the landscape. A house to sell to the highest bidder, generating revenue for investment in the big mansion was repeated, preventing awkward questions.

Moving in was a masterpiece of logistics. Their personal effects were removed in the dead of night, furniture with sleight of hand, disappeared, replaced as if by magic. Every effort to keep their secret was enacted with military precision.

The house looked wonderful and Jess's happiness knew no bounds. The sight of her toddler trying hard to walk and Sebastian's pride growing with her every step, Pricilla Jane (Prissy) was the light of their lives.

As their wedding date approached, Jess was the happiest she had ever been. Her excitement was infectious and everyone gloried in her joy.

Relaxed in their newfound happiness, they were reluctant to rake up old feelings of concern the unexpected birth would create.

Prissy jumped for joy seeing her new bedroom and Sebastian made love to Jess with passion like never before in their four-poster bed.

A new home, a new little girl, almost married to the most beautiful woman in the world. What could exceed his joy? Sebastian was on top of the world.

Days turned to weeks in a haze of contentment Jess had never experienced before. Moving effortlessly from her wonderful home to the brothel each day was heaven on earth.

No one seemed to notice Jess's disappearance early evening to put Prissy to bed with a cuddle and kiss goodnight or her return to begin a night of joy entertaining her clientele. The late nights and days spent with Sebastian and Prissy a pleasure like none other, Jess's world was complete.

The letter of reconciliation to her mom and dad returned to sender was no surprise. "I bet if he knew I was a millionaire, his answer would be different," she looked sadly towards Chris, who was privy to her 'unfortunate circumstances' (Chris's words, not hers). "I'm well rid of them." She finally grinned, burning the letter over the waste bin. "Cancel their invite!" she added. "Their loss, not mine."

"The one we haven't sent out yet?" Chris joined in.

Both girls with similar circumstances, neither had parents who understood their daughters. Jess and Julia had forged a relationship and no sisters could be closer.

Sebastian's family had softened slightly to their wayward son and when he explained he was to marry an extremely rich young lady (not how she achieved it), they seemed to warm to the idea.

A second date was discussed for the wedding and this time, the planners pencilled in the date with a proviso of should it be delayed again, a forfeit would be imposed.

"No need to worry about this!" Jess said, filing her letter of agreement under wedding arrangements. "It's a sure thing this time. No need to hide from anyone." Jess delighted they had succeeded in achieving a miracle.

***

The shock when Sebastian announced, "You will be proud of me!" as he searched the safe for his passport. "I have a contract to photograph the wedding of the century!" He boasted, feeling elated that, at last, his efforts to win a life-changing contract had succeeded.

Jess studied his face. "And this contract is where?" was her question, knowing it was overseas didn't need a crystal ball.

"St Lucia! An old colleague recommended me. I hadn't seen him in years, but his friend, a rock star of great wealth, is finally marrying his long-suffering girlfriend." Sebastian continued his good fortune without looking around.

Jess stood mortified as he continued to search his wardrobes. "I may need to replace some of these," he said, throwing a selection of his pre-Jess sun wear onto the bed.

The slammed door should have been a clue she was less than happy with his 'good fortune', but as he'd worked tirelessly to get his foundling business off the ground, he didn't get the significance of her flounce. "Be down in a minute!" he called after her, lifting his case from the closet.

Humming a familiar Bajan ditty, Sebastian was still fully concentrated as Jess turned the handle of their bedroom door. "And when is this little gem going to happen?" Jess questioned.

Still, the attitude failed to hit the mark. "The beginning of next month. I must crack on. It's only a week away. It's a brilliant opportunity for my business to get off the ground. This guy knows everybody who's somebody all over the world. It's so exciting, Jess…" He turned, stopping in his tracks as the stone-faced look from Jess threw ice water all over him.

"What?" Sebastian asked, a shrug of the shoulders, totally bewildered, having no idea where this was coming from.

"You're just flying off to the Caribbean without giving me or Prissy a second thought?" Jess's question was loaded with sarcasm.

"I thought you'd be pleased for me. It's a great opportunity…" Before he could continue, Jess burst into tears.

It took a while, but finally the penny dropped. "Jess, you know how much I wanted this. It's not just for me but for all of us!" His words sounded hollow the more Jess sobbed.

"I don't want it. It's 'your baby'," she shouted. "Why didn't you tell me you had visions of grandeur?"

The barb hit the spot, forcing Sebastian to retaliate, "What do you mean grandeur? This has long been my ambition and you know it. I have no intention of glorying in your limelight…." His words petered as the echo of the past returned. "I'm sorry, Jess, I didn't mean…" Before he could explain, the door closed, but this time quietly.

"To hell with everything," he slammed the lid on his case and made for the stairs.

"She's in the garden!" Julia pointed to the lake, unaware of the altercation.

"Thanks, Julia," Sebastian mumbled, wondering how he would calm the waters this time.

"Please!" Jess said, as he approached looking hangdog. "I know exactly why you're going!"

"Yes and I'm aware you have reservations, but you should know by now how much I love you," his words fell on deaf ears. "Please try to understand this in no way means I don't love you. Quite the opposite. I want to be part of the team doing something I care about just as much as you do here with Julia."

Sitting in a wisteria-covered alcove did nothing to soften Jess's stance. "How long before the 'Dear John' letter arrives when you get in with your cronies?" She'd changed from sobs to stone.

"They're not cronies. They're genuinely nice people who respect what I do!" He had no idea what to say to console her. "The strength of a man is not the muscles he bears, it's the fortitude in which he carries out his life." Sebastian, losing the battle, was determined to win the war.

Jess stared straight ahead. "Says who, your posh friends?" Jess retorted, trying to hide her heartache.

No more pandering, Sebastian walked away. Not looking back, he secretly hoped Jess would follow. He had another weapon to use in the fight for financial independence. He was sure she loved him as he loved her and given a chance, he would demonstrate how much.

The no show scared him. "Julia, have you seen Jess?"

"She went to town and took Prissy with her. Not sure where to. She didn't say!" Seeing his distress, Julia realised all was not good in the love birds' household. "Problems in paradise?" she questioned, hoping to play devil's advocate.

"I have secured a photography contract for a wedding. That's not all. It's in St Lucia and I will possibly be away for a month!" saying the words made him understand Jess's reaction.

"Hmm, I can see why that would go down like a lead-welly," Julia sighed. "What do you plan to do?"

"There's nothing I can do. I've signed the contract. A very lucrative contract as it happens." Sebastian could now see why Jess was upset. "Would you have a word with her? Explain it's best for both of us to have different interests?"

Julia threw up her hands, "Sorry, my friend, that would only make it worse. Jess hates interference. Trust me."

In some ways, Julia knew Jess better than anyone. "She will come around. Her reaction is probably twofold. One, she loves you and doesn't want you to go away. And two, it's to where you first met, which rings lots of alarm bells."

Bombarded with instructions and plans to make for the 'once in a lifetime event', the bride explained it as 'the most memorable event on the calendar'. *"Don't worry, Daddy will settle the account promptly following the deposit which is enclosed."* Her handwriting displayed her educational origins and the envelope stated, 'By Royal Appointment,' which spoke volumes.

For Sebastian, this was life changing. Once on the society bandwagon, it would be plain sailing. The one thing he didn't want was for anything to go wrong.

It wasn't a lot to ask. A few weeks, maybe a month at the outside, away from Jess and Prissy. Why was she making it so difficult for him when he'd supported her one hundred percent from the day they met? It didn't make sense.

"One bloody month," he cursed under his breath. Well, it was done and he couldn't get out even had he wanted to, which he didn't. Sebastian made a pact not to be influenced by anyone, this was 'his day' and he intended to see it through no matter what.

He sat for hours pondering the outcome of his relationship with Jess. He loved her desperately, but he was a man, after all, and men were the breadwinners. Weren't they?

The questions reverberated until he decided to have one last try to make amends.

"Come with me like we agreed. We could make it a holiday," his plea seemed weak compared to what he would have said had he had time to rehearse.

"Are you insane? Leave the business at its busiest to take Prissy to a country reaching more than 35 degrees? Where are your brains? In your pants like every other male?" Jess was still livid he chose to cavort across the world when there was no need.

"Stop now, Jess! You know that's not true. I have signed a contract, which could break me if I renege," Sebastian raising his voice emotionally.

"You should have thought of that before signing." There was no getting away from the fact that Jess's mind was made up that he was wrong.

His attempt to kiss her was shrugged aside, "Save it for your next floozy!" her retort cutting through his heart.

Turning to leave, distraught by her rebuttal, Sebastian left with a lump in his throat. "And don't come back!" Jess screamed, slamming the door behind him.

Falling to the bed, Jess sobbed. Nothing, it would seem, could convince him not to go. *What will I do without you?* she howled like a wolf losing a pup.

"He's gone!" Julia murmured when Jess finally left her room.

"What have I done?" Jess was still traumatised by her anger.

"It didn't go well, I take it. He left without a word," Julia fibbed. The kiss on her cheek and his fond farewell were a complete surprise. The piece of paper he left in her hand, even more so. His address and a message, "Keep in touch," dumfounded Julia. She read it over and over, wondering if it was meant for Jess, but clearly, the "Thank you, Julia, for everything," was a reality check.

It was obvious he had hoped she would pass it on to Jess when the furore died down. Wasn't it?

Chapter Twenty-Eight

The next few days were hell. Moving from one emotion to another, a state of catatonic oblivion one minute, hysterics the next, it was obvious to Julia something was drastically wrong. Mulling around, even Prissy's attempt to get her attention went unnoticed. "Mommy, when's Daddy coming home?" only made things worse.

"How would I know?" the blunt unexpected retort made Prissy cry.

"Jess that was out of order!" Julia rebuked, "Prissy misses him as much as you do!"

"Who says I miss him? If he cared at all, he wouldn't have left." Burying her head in her hands, Jess sobbed uncontrollably.

The postcard saying, 'Wish you were here' was torn to shreds and binned before the words were read. His pleading for her to join him, bringing Prissy and her nanny on a private plane, lay torn to pieces unanswered.

Julia retrieved the fragments. Placing them carefully on a table, she tried once more to convince her. "Come on, Jess, see it from his point of view!" was dismissed with a grunt.

"Dear Julia,
I take it Jess is not joining me! I'm broken-hearted and unable to enjoy what should have been the best time of my life, except for being with Jess and Prissy, of

course. Is there a way you could persuade her and come
along with them yourself? I will be eternally grateful.
   Best,
   Sebastian"

It wasn't rocket-science. Jess would fly into a
tantrum should she even approach the subject. "Jess,
love, I know you're hurting. Sebastian is too. He's asked
for you to join him, bringing me and Prissy along, if you
can find it in your heart to forgive him?"

"Go! Take Prissy with you. See if I care. You'll
see I'm right. He's cavorting with other women as we
speak!" Jess said, flouncing from the room. Julia feared
for Jess's stability.

Having lost weight, drinking to excess every night,
flirting with the punters, it was if she was in self-destruct
mode and Julia was unable to console her. "Ok, I'll take
Prissy and check if you're right," Julia said, hoping this
would spur her into relenting, not meaning a word.

The frenzy and raging expletives followed by
sobbing, slamming doors and throwing things, then by a
weird silence, was almost too much for Julia to bear.

"Calm down, you'll have a breakdown!" Julia's
attempt to shock her out of her hysteria with a slap, did
the opposite.

"Bitch!" Jess hollered, stopped and, with a look of
unfretted torment, ran from the room.

"I didn't mean to hurt you!" Julia was horrified Jess had mistaken her action. "It's the only way I know to halt a breakdown," she pleaded to deaf ears.

Days passed and Jess walked around zombified. Chris, aware of the catastrophic effect Sebastian's leaving had wrought upon his dearest friend and confidant, began to closely watch over her.

"Would you care to ride today? The air is fresh and a change of scenery would do you and your horse good." Chris did his best to comfort her.

"What use is anything anymore?" her past bringing forward an unhealthy negativity.

"Prissy would love it. Her new pony needs a workout." He tried in vain, using her daughter he felt sure would bring her around.

"Tell Julia, not me. She seems to be Sebastian's 'go-to-girl' these days." Her sarcasm shocked him.

"Rubbish, we're all trying to help." Chris was horrified Jess was using Julia to make her point.

A lifetime of disappointment and struggling constantly to keep the status quo had taken its toll and Sebastian leaving seemed to be the final straw.

"What are we to do? I fear for her sanity," Chris asked, panicked, concern written all over his face.

Having known Jess's resilience over the years and her ability to see the long game by pushing the negative from her mind and soldiering on, Julia was lost for words. "Why now, after all she's been through in the past?" Julia queried.

"Perhaps it's time to contact Sebastian?" Chris suggested. "Do you think he would come back?"

"He's tied to a contract, so to do so would be a financial catastrophe. We need to get Jess over there to see for herself."

Deciding to leave well enough alone for the time being, Julia and Chris struggled on as if Jess was fine until Sebastian called.

Out riding or shopping they explained, or as many excuses as they could come up with. Meanwhile, Jess became more unreasonable, refusing to take his calls, throwing the telephone through the window in an out-of-control temper, followed by hours looking through unseeing eyes through the window.

"Where's Mommy? Is she coming to kiss me good night?" Prissy asked her nanny, who had grown more and more worried her charge was being rejected.

"I'm sure she'll be here soon. Just close your eyes for a moment…." Nanny kissed Prissy gently, hoping her words were true.

The morning made matters worse, "Mommy, Mommy, where were you? I closed my eyes like Nanny said, but you didn't come." Jess resisted despite Prissy pushing her arm. Finally, holding her mom's hand, Prissy whispered, "Are you poorly, Mommy?"

The hungover reply made her daughter cry, "Go tell Aunty Julia, not me. I no longer care." Jess turned over as Prissy stood sobbing.

Julia was told of Jess's latest outburst. "What in God's name do you think you're doing?" she shook Jess awake.

"F… off, it's nothing to do with you," her reply shocked Julia into action.

"Doctor, can you come over? I'm afraid Jess is really ill." What she wanted to say is, "The bitch wants a good hiding for hurting her daughter's feelings," but kept her wrath under check, wondering if Jess was far worse than anyone thought.

Doctor Winston was a wonderful man, kind, caring and extremely good at his job. Although he would have explained, "It's not a job, it's a vocation," as serving his patients was his life's ambition.

Seeing Jess changed from a happy, healthy young woman he'd attended during her pregnancy to seeing her now a bundle of bones smelling of alcohol and goodness knows what, he immediately suggested some time in a rest home would be best.

"You mean put her away?" Julia was horrified, but at the same time, if it would bring the old Jess back, it would be worth it.

Having explained Mommy was poorly and the doctor had suggested she go to hospital to make her well, "Can I go with her? She needs me," the little girl said, tears streaming down her face.

Prissy, although young, understood being ill and what it meant for her mom. Having held her hand as the

236

doctor administered a sedative when the ambulance arrived, she dried her tears and, turning to Julia, smiled. "She'll be better soon. The doctor said so!"

Not long now before Sebastian came home, the extension for pictures of the bride and groom's honeymoon had seen extra weeks added for a bounty he considered worthwhile. Although Jess had replied, "Do what you want," putting down the phone before he could explain the advantages, he felt sure when she saw the presents he had carefully chosen for her and Prissy, she would be over the moon.

Realising the mistake of no communication of the true facts, Julia decided to wait until almost the end of his follow up contract before telling Sebastian the truth. "She's not answered my letters and won't speak on the phone. I've spoken to Chris and you more times than Jess. What's going on?"

"She's still cross and misses you like mad, but you know Jess. She'd rather say nothing than tell you her true feelings." The explanation sounded thin considering the extent of her present state.

***

Warm sun and stunning views, the Seychelle Islands were the perfect location for Sebastian's talent as a photographer.

Looking into each other's eyes, their love light shone through. The pictures he took of the bride and groom were his best yet. "I love them," the bride romanced as the dollars rolled in with every masterpiece.

Jess would see it was best for them both. Feeling better the more his bank balance grew, he would never meet her wealth, but his contribution to their future looked set to rise with every recommendation.

The list of contacts swelled and, although more travel would be involved, he felt sure when he explained to Jess what the value his financial independence meant to him, she would welcome the efforts he made for them both.

The heady nights dancing under the stars, his popularity growing with every picture he took, Sebastian never lost sight of the love he felt for Jess.

"Just fun," he explained to the party girls. "I'm married and have a wonderful daughter," was his reaction when the heat was turned up for more.

This was business no matter the temptation and he would return to the love of his life as soon as the photo-shoot was over.

Little did he know of the despair Jess was going through since he left or the drastic measures needed as a consequence.

Julia had no idea how to explain Jess not being at the airport to welcome him or the ongoing treatment she would need before returning to full health. It was a nightmare with no end in sight.

Days passed and Sebastian would soon be home. Head in hands, Julia rehearsed the script.

All thoughts of what or not what to say to Sebastian left her mind the moment she watched as he came through arrivals, looking brown and twice as handsome as she remembered.

Tears welled as he looked around for Jess. "Daddy," Prissy, arms outstretched temporarily took his attention with a big hug. "Mommy's poorly," she shouted before Julia had a chance to explain.

"Oh," he murmured, looking over the hug into Julia's eyes.

"But the doctor says she'll be better soon," Prissy added as Julia shrugged, her despair obvious.

Carefully releasing Prissy, Sebastian turned. "I'll explain later," Julia tried a smile as his daughter took his hand, tugging in the direction of the limousine.

Incredulous, Sebastian sat, awaiting familiar surroundings. Although the journey from the airport was free of the normal rush-hour traffic, it seemed hours before they arrived home.

"What's going on? Why didn't you tell me Jess was sick. Which hospital?" he added, placing his luggage in the hallway and Prissy in the capable hands of her nanny.

"It's not a hospital as such, more a recovery facility!" Julia tried to rosy a difficult conversation.

"And what does that mean exactly?" He was irritated by not being told of her illness, but also suspected Julia was lying.

"The doctor feared for her mental health!" Julia replied, still unable to say institutionalised for her own good.

"In a mental health facility?" Sebastian was outraged. "You should have informed me, Julia. What were you thinking?"

"You were miles away. What good would it have done? It was because you went away she had a breakdown." Not wishing him to think it her fault, the words came out unexpectedly harsh.

"Oh my God. I had no idea!" he sat head in hands.

"Sorry, Sebastian, it was not just down to you. Jess had many obstacles to climb over the years and the thought you preferred to stay away was the last in a long line of disappointments." Julia's rehearsed script totally shot, she hoped he understood.

"My poor darling. Take me there at once," having found Sandy. "Please and be quick."

The agony of the journey, Julia insisting she go along, was the worst in his life. "I can't believe she would think me so shallow. I love her so. I told her a million times." He hesitated, tears filling his eyes.

"Like I say, it's not all down to you. Jess suffered many let-downs. Losing you was the worst."

"But I would never abandon her. I thought she knew that!"

Julia felt desperately sorry for them both. "Words are cheap when they're said many times without substance," she added, wishing she had the answer.

"How long has she been...... ill?"

"She deteriorated after you extended your stay. It seemed to confirm her worst nightmares. Even Prissy couldn't help." Julia began to sob, "I'm not sure what can be done."

"I will make her see!" confident he would be bringing her home, Sebastian soldiered on.

"Please, can I see her doctor? Jess and I were about to marry," he asked the ward sister.

Shaking her head, "It's too soon. Jess has been sedated and it may be some time before she's allowed visitors." She looked sympathetic as he turned to leave.

"I'm not a visitor. I love her and she loves me. Don't you see? Had I stayed, she would not have...." he stopped in his tracks as her doctor arrived.

"See for yourself," Jess's doctor pointed to her room through the window.

Chapter Twenty-Nine

Despite the final payment arriving on the day the bridegroom promised, it seemed petty by comparison to what had happened since his return.

All the 'if onlys' in the world wouldn't change Jess's plight and a mixture of regret and sadness followed Sebastian around like a bad smell.

The memory of their meeting and the romance that followed stayed with him wherever he went. He clung to each moment they spent together, wishing he could take a step back from his ambition.

Seeing Jess lying in the psychiatric hospital oblivious to the world was the worst time in his life.

He knew he had to console Prissy, although he was unable to be consoled. Sitting at his desk, hands shaking, Sebastian asked himself as he folded the apology letters, *How many more times will our wedding be postponed?*

What would happen to Jess's part in the business, he had no idea! Julia had been a rock. Chris and the other loyal employees, even the more recent staff, had pulled together, keeping the clients in the dark as to her illness.

Although Jess was out of bed, her blank stare and incessant rocking did nothing to inspire Sebastian's confidence she would soon be well.

His constant assurance that he loved her and always would fell on deaf ears. Even Prissy, on the occasions her mom was more responsive, failed to dispel her malaise.

"When will Mommy be better?" her question was unable to be answered by not only Sebastian, but the doctor was reluctant to speculate.

Detached from normal situations, Jess remained unresponsive. "It will take time. We must have patience. Even the strongest recover slowly from a breakdown," the doctors confirmed.

Helpless was not a word Sebastian had been familiar with until now. As each day passed, his resilience waned. Being strong for Prissy when he needed every ounce of strength himself was the hardest challenge of all.

The world around him seemed to move on regardless of his despair. Clients came and left, Julia smiled when asked the whereabouts of her dear friend, "A long stay holiday, lucky devil," she joked, hoping to be believed.

Accepting it would take time, Sebastian soldiered on. Taking on only local, more lucrative contracts, wedding photography was the hardest. His and Jess's postponement now being permanently on hold, weddings forced painful memories to return.

The most terrifying was not knowing how, if ever, Jess would return to her old self. All the money in the world couldn't compensate for the agony of losing the love of his life. Not in the traditional way, where people fall out of love, but a more devastating reality that Jess may never feel the same even if she recovered.

"There must be something more we can do. Maybe a convalescent home in Switzerland?" Sebastian despaired of Jess's limp hands as he held them and her pale, unrecognising face looking back at him.

He was grasping at straws following the 'heart to heart' with her latest specialist, who confirmed the only thing to do was to wait and see. "Let the drugs do the work," he insisted, seeing a look on Jess's face he was now familiar with.

"We can't leave it here!" Sebastian murmured to Julia. Despairing of the prognosis, he insisted they speak to one of Jess's clients who practised psychiatry.

Having listened to Sebastian's pleading, 'a better, speedier solution may be found by introducing new ideas,' Julia hesitated, "You understand the implications as we run a brothel?"

"Surely as a consultant psychiatrist, his first loyalty is to his patient?" Sebastian responded.

Following research into Sir Patrick, Julia agreed to try. "He's a very smart guy. Although he seeks his sexual pleasures outside the marital bed, he's obliged to keep his professional life separate."

Thinking on his feet, Sebastian replied, "Also, he wouldn't want his own dalliance to be discovered," positive it was the right decision.

The extra attention Julia showered on Sir Patrick was intended to discover which area of mental health he practiced.

Although Sebastian was impatient to get to the point, Julia felt they needed to know more, "Suppose he only treats children or the elderly? It would be pointless involving him, which may jeopardise our position."

He was eager to see the love of his life restored. "To hell with our position. I want her back!" Sebastian raged and cried at the same time, unable to see the point of living without her.

"I'm sorry, Sebastian, it was thoughtless of me," Julia despaired. "I was thinking of the many lives that depend on our business."

"There's nothing to forgive. I know how much Jess means to you," Sebastian's humble stance said it all.

On their frequent visits, Prissy held Jess's hand. Talking incessantly about her day at school and what happened in the playground, it was heartbreaking how she now took for granted her mom's silence. "See you tomorrow," she smiled, kissing her mom gently.

"What will I do without her?" Sebastian, desperate for a sign, murmured.

Confident they had the right man for the job, "I will approach Sir Patrick tonight," Julia whispered. "I'm sure he will try."

Sir Patrick O'Shaughnessy was an upright, staunch member of the psychiatric upper echelon who had no idea of his unusual sexual habits. Thankfully, this trait had been successfully hidden from his family and inner sanctum over the years.

Few at J&J's knew of his unorthodox preferences and they wouldn't tell for fear of their own habits being divulged.

Not forgetting Julia, Jess, and the girls he now called by their first names, and Sebastian added to his list of friends, Sir Patrick, they hoped, would be the answer to their prayers.

A vision of him flaunting his family on royal occasions, boasting his prowess with his wife to his friends when spending his nights with their floozy's. It had always been a mystery to Julia, not that she didn't understand. It was how their business survived.

She smiled, thinking of the peculiarities of her clients. The girls' stories were the bedrock of their profession and their clients' secrets were kept without question.

Their business was successful, their punters were happy and their wealth exceeded all expectations. What good was it now with Jess so ill?

"A watched pot never boils," was how Chris phrased it, as night after night they looked out for Sir Patrick to arrive.

Friday night late, Sir Patrick's familiar stance, shrugged-off caped coat (reminiscent of Sherlock Holmes), black and red spotted bow tie, a signature stamp of 'top dog', a wink at the first girl that caught his eye, and Julia rushed to his side. "Can we speak privately?"

Nudge-nudge, wink-wink, "Am I in for a treat?" his cheeky grin was followed by a grimace from Julia. "Oh dear, am I in trouble?" Sir Patrick added, seeing her worried face.

"No, no, I just need to run something by you. Professionally, you understand!" Julia not wanting him to think otherwise.

"How can I help?" he questioned as he settled into a comfy leather chair, removing his pretend one eye spectacle.

"It's Jess!" Julia stuttered. "She's ill and we think you can help!"

"I thought I hadn't seen her lately. Has she seen a doctor?"

Julia hesitated, "Your profession is what she needs. She is in the care of a psychiatric facility, but we understand you have methods other than drugs?"

Unsure of her next words, Julia faltered. "She's been in a catatonic state for some time and we had hoped you could think of a solution?"

"Hmm, I would need to see her as a patient," his look stern. "You understand, it would be unprofessional to intervene without her doctor's and her family's consent."

Julia, not having thought of Jess's family, lied, "I have no recollection of Jess's family. Sebastian, as you know, is her intended. They have a daughter together but she's too young to offer her consent. We are desperate. Is there nothing you can do?"

"I will approach her specialist and see if he will agree to me seeing her." He shook his head, "Who would have thought it? Jess seemed so strong!"

"It's a long story, I'm afraid, but like most outwardly strong people, sometimes their background can be a stumbling block."

Thanking him profusely, Julia shook his hand, "Money's no object…" she began as he looked pensive.

"This one's on me," Sir Patrick touched the side of his nose. "No promises, mind, it all depends on her specialist. He may be protective of his patient."

Realising the implication of his comment, Julia offered up, "We are extremely wealthy. I'm sure you can persuade him?" Almost bowing at the waist, Julia took his hand longer than necessary, "We will be eternally grateful."

As he turned to leave for his night of pleasure, Julia called out, "Sir Partick. This ones on me!"

***

Agreeing in principle, Jess's specialist considered the possibilities. It had been practised many times in America by top psychiatric practitioners in the sixties and seventies, considering it a short sharp solution when drugs seemed a more long-term and a less effective remedy.

Much was discussed behind closed doors, fearing the impact of the procedure on some patients being less effective than others.

"More needs to be done in this field before I give my sanction," her specialist insisted. Not the overwhelming consent Sebastian expected.

Although controversial in many ways, the benefits of electroconvulsive therapy had been swifter and successful.

"Don't you see? Your drugs don't seem to be working. The more Jess sits vegetating, the more Sir Patrick's methods seem the answer," Sebastian pleaded, desperate for a solution to Jess's malaise.

Consultations and meetings with many in the field of psychiatry took place before being convinced Jess's controversial practitioner take over her treatment.

Realising many cases had been hailed a success, her current specialist finally relented, shaking Sir Patrick's hand in a gesture of, "I hope all goes well."

"I'll do my best. Thank you for your trust." Sir Patrick returned his handshake, as the pair of highly trained and proficient in the world of mental illness went their separate ways.

Promising to contact him through his clinic with the results, Sir Partick O'Shaughnessy made plans to move Jess to his clinic in hills looking over spectacular views without delay.

Their visits were curtailed until all preparations were complete. Prissy was confused and upset. "Why can't I visit Mommy? Is she more poorly?" her question was heart rendering as she clutched a bunch of wild flowers picked for her regular visit.

"No, Mommy's been moved for special care. We hope it will help bring her home sooner," Sebastian added as Prissy's lip dropped. "Don't be sad, she will be back in time to see you jump your new pony. If you try really hard, it will seem no time at all," he said with a tear in his eye, hoping it to be true.

Jess's room was palatial. Although no recognition of the journey or her surroundings, Sebastian was satisfied everything that could be done would be carried out with care and consideration of her complex condition.

"She won't feel a thing," Sir Patrick tried to convince Sebastian. "A general anaesthetic will be carried out before the procedure." He hesitated, "Please rest assured she is in the best hands."

Assisting Sebastian into a lounge fit for royalty, he called for tea. "Or something stronger?" Sir Patrick questioned, seeing the state of concern he harboured.

Having stayed in far less attractive hotels, Sebastian rang to speak to Julia. "She's comfortable. They will be starting the procedure shortly. She won't feel anything…." He found it hard to continue.

"Thank God. I've been worried and so has Prissy," a sob caught in Julia's throat.

"Is she there? I'll try to put her mind to rest," Sebastian added, composure a must to convince her all was well, although his knuckles were white from a clenched fist.

"Hello, darling, Mommy's fine. The doctor's with her at the moment giving her medicine to make her better."

"I don't like medicine," Prissy answered, thinking of the linctus for her cough.

Sebastian found it hard to speak without giving away his concern. "It's to make Mommy well again, so I don't think she minds," he added, holding back the tears.

"Tell her I love her and come home soon," she said, a sadness in her voice he recognised well.

"I will, my darling. I'll see you tomorrow. Love you!" he said, hoping he had convinced her, although he remained concerned.

Chapter Thirty

"Complications? What complications?" Sebastian's anger and frustration was obvious. "For God's sake, random, how can an inspection be random?"

Although no one spoke, the situation became clear. A piece of paper holding up the procedure until a family member by marriage or parentage could be established giving consent, the whole thing was cancelled.

Head down, Sir Patrick slunk to his room. His reputation sullied by his deliberate attempt to bypass the rules would take years to restore, if ever. Not forgetting the poor girl anesthetized in readiness for her life to be restored.

In his anger towards the self-righteous, self-serving bigot, the guy with a holier-than-thou attitude who had forced the love of his life to suffer on indefinitely was too much for Sebastian to bear.

Wanting to use brute force, a good hiding seeming a good idea, a swift grip of Sebastian's arm and a face almost too close to Mr 'whatever his name is' was halted by her specialist. "That will do no one any good, least of all Jess," he intervened.

The facility's inspector's strong, gym induced, hand preventing what could have been a catastrophe, added, "Rules are rules. If you know what's good for your girlfriend, you will abide by the statute book."

Nodding to the doorman to unlock the door, the puffed-up bureaucrat with no sympathy for Jess's well-being awaited the council's chauffeur to open the door of his tax-funded limousine.

"Ticking boxes is all you're good for!" Sebastian hollered after him, banging his hand on the door as it slammed shut. "Where do her parents live?" he shouted at Julia, feeling out of control.

"I think the address is in her office. I'm not sure. We never spoke of them after a brief exchange when we met. They washed their hands of her years ago." Julia began to cry.

"I'll find them somehow," Sebastian ranted, running from the facility without looking back.

The municipalities were next. It hadn't occurred to Sebastian or Julia that her parents may have moved. "Excuse me, could you please tell me where this family lives? I need to explain their eldest daughter's in hospital?" He held out the piece of paper.

Although the address given was clear, they had obviously moved on due to financial reasons.

The dilapidated cottage-style three bed, one bathroom house, although in a rural area, was now empty awaiting the next buyer. Jess's family were nowhere to be found.

Returning to the fool who could not read, Sebastian was incandescent despite the housing operative still having her parents on his register.

"They've been re-housed," he turned the pages. "Housed in a more compact subsidised apartment on an estate more suitable to their needs." The half-asleep individual, more interested in his sandwich box than caring a damn, yawned.

"I'll stuff that sandwich where the sun doesn't shine if you don't give me their new address. Do you understand me?" Sebastian's stance, eye to eye, did the trick.

"Sorry," he mumbled, pulling out their family file and writing down their new address.

Without another word, Sebastian and Julia sped off in the general direction. "It must be here somewhere!" Julia said, checking the local map.

Having driven around for what seemed like forever, "Do you think the idiot has a clue where they are? I think he wrote the first address down he could think of." Ready to return and rip off his head, Sebastian thumped the steering wheel.

Driving through an obvious slum with broken down cars, bins overflowing, drunks slumped in doorways, the estate had them all. "Surely this can't be the place?" Julia questioned seeing kids fighting in the street.

"If it is, they've fallen on more than hard times. This is rock bottom," Sebastian said unable to catch a breath.

Stretching his neck through the open window, Sebastian pointed to the top floor of an apartment block. "It's up there!" he said, hoping not.

"OMG," Julia exclaimed as Sebastian parked in a space for number 203.

As expected, the lift was out. Graffiti confirming 'Ban the bomb' and some other expletives they had no knowledge of, the pair began the upward trek that would hopefully solve the problem. "I'm telling you, Julia, if they so much as hesitate to sign, I will swing for them."

With his hackles still up from his encounter with the miserable son of a bitch in subsidised housing doing nothing to calm his nerves, he strode upwards as if demented.

"Please calm down. We need them to understand how difficult Jess's situation is and persuasion is better than force under the circumstances," Julia pleaded.

The knock on the door was loud. The answer, "What'd want?" did nothing to calm their anxiety.

"Mr Turner? I'm Sebastian, a close friend of your daughter Jessica and I'm with her friend Julia. I wonder if you could help us?" He managed to keep his tone in check as he spoke through the door.

"She isn't here. We haven't seen her since she became highfalutin." The door flung open. "She has no need for us, so what do you want?" It was more a command than a question and Sebastian feared the worst.

"Jess is not well and needs an operation, but we need a signature before the doctor will operate," Julia, trying to keep it simple, added with a weak smile.

"She's of age. So why should you need us to help?" the question led to a more in-depth explanation.

"She's unconscious," Sebastian jumped in not wanting to divulge the truth to this uncouth moron.

"What's she done, tumbled from her money tree?" Sarcasm not the best answer, Julia thought, as Sebastian fought to hold his temper.

"They think she has a brain bleed, so it's very urgent," Julia interrupted.

"What's it worth?" His grin was worthy of a smack. Sebastian reached for his wallet.

Jess's father's opportunist attitude when his daughter was so desperately ill infuriated an already 'at the end of his tether' Sebastian. "How much to salve your conscience?" he growled, holding out a wadge of dollars without checking. Red in the face, he threw the bribe down.

"Give the bloody thing here and begone. Don't give her our love and don't come here again," Jess's father took the pen and scribbled his name.

Seeing Jess's mom in tears, Julia realised her father's reaction wasn't shared. "Please give her a chance," she begged her husband as he pushed her to one side.

Julia, although upset by his anger, sighed with relief as Sebastian snatched the paper before her father changed his mind.

Slamming the door behind them, "I would have strangled the bastard had he refused," Sebastian said through gritted teeth, taking the stairs two at a time. They made for the car and a way out of the maze of deprivation.

"It's not as simple as that!" Sir Patrick said, sounding sad.

"Why? I did as you asked." Sebastian threw his hands in the air.

Thinking before he answered, "I broke the rules and it's very serious. Should I fail......" he tried to explain, embarrassment all over his face.

"Serious for you? What about Jess?" Feeling his blood pressure rise, Sebastian sat down head in hands.

Seeing the strength of his pain, Sir Patrick placed a hand on his shoulder. "I have a plan!"

Sir Patrick suggested that he guide Jess's specialist through the procedure, having convinced him it would work. He posed as a mature student under supervision. Although unorthodox, Sir Patrick's reputation as mentor and teacher being renowned and with his guiding hand and impeccable instincts, her specialist was happy to proceed.

He felt the need to explain the detail, "Electroconvulsive therapy normally requires four to six treatments before a successful conclusion can be confirmed and it will take approximately three to four weeks to complete.

"We can, however, expect to see an improvement in the first week with a gradual advancement over the following weeks." Sir Patrick, eager to clarify his knowledge, concluded.

Under his careful direction, the first treatment began. Sir Patrick, having explained the risks and benefits for most patients, Jess's specialist took control.

More fraught than when Jess was having Prissy, Sebastian paced and wrung his hands as if at the birth as a first-time father.

It seemed forever before the pair alighted the fully equipped surgery. Shaking hands, they made for the luxurious waiting room. The whole setup reeked of wealth. Overlooking a lake complete with a fountain to calm the nerves, it was a world away from the normal setting of a hospital. Rather than the traditional smell of antiseptic, a fragrance of roses and lavender filled the air, but did nothing to alleviate their concern.

Had Sebastian not been frantic with anticipation of the outcome, he would have thought it a luxurious stately home. Having sat silently awaiting the outcome, he rose anxiously as Sir Patrick entered.

"Is she ok? Can I see her?" were Sebastian's first words, perspiration on his forehead despite the fresh air.

"We must leave her until the anaesthetic wears off and she's had her first examination. It shouldn't be long, but you must be aware Jess may be a little confused to

258

begin with and it will take time for the results to be assessed," Sir Patrick cautioned.

The advice they go home and come back tomorrow was refused with contrition. "If it's ok with you, we would prefer to stay?" Sebastian's look of sorry pressing home his concern.

He and Julia sat without speaking. No words would be of use. It was as if the whole world was turning as theirs stood still.

Having spent the night watching the door, it was late afternoon the next day before the sister beckoned. "Just one at a time. She's not fully awake." Turning, she guided Sebastian to a grandiose suite with facilities to challenge royalty.

Holding her hand for what seemed like an age, Sebastian prayed silently.

A tear unnoticed as he sat thinking of the past. "Will the passion we shared be restored?" he asked himself before looking lovingly into her face.

"Doctor, come quick!" he called out.

Chapter Thirty-One

Jess's recovery, although slow at first, was hastened by the attention from her beloved Sebastian, Prissy, Julia, Chris and her other close friends. No looking back, they began life after her treatment as if the past months hadn't happened.

Work for Jess started again. Everyone at the brothel was happy to have her back at the helm, thinking she had arrived from a holiday of a lifetime, the fib believed by all but her nearest and dearest.

Julia, seeing her friend almost back to normal, was ecstatic. Nothing more would be said even as an afterthought of her 'blip' as they called it. Her recovery was even more remarkable than even her specialist had predicted.

Sebastian took only photography contracts within an acceptable distance from their home, enabling him to return each evening no matter what. No nights away unless Jess agreed to join him. It was a perfect solution to his now flourishing business and Jess's newfound happy disposition.

Life was good settled in their new mansion, everything in place for a happy ever after. Jess made giant strides back to her old self.

Sir Patrick, sworn to secrecy, even his family was excluded, as were his nightly visits to J&J's. He smiled, seeing the result of his magic, his name intact due to

Jess's specialist's expertise, learning quickly and with a precision many qualified psychiatric practitioners wished they possessed.

A party in her honour and a new date set for their wedding, the wedding dress out of its trunk for the umpteenth time, the limousine polished to its pearlized perfection, the grandest reception rescheduled, what more could they want.

"Sebastian, I have an idea!" Jess said casually, having opened her hospital file.

She was surprised to read the consent form signed by her father, inwardly digesting Sebastian's version of how grateful he and Julia were for his help. Not the real version, 'I could have happily strangled the bastard for not wanting to sign'. It seemed kinder to offer a more conducive explanation to secure Jess's happy disposition.

Julia made it worse, having explained her family's misfortune. "I've made up my mind. I want to buy our old place." Jess hummed, "I've given lots of thought as to how I can heal my relationship with my family and restoring their old cottage seems a perfect opportunity."

Sebastian, shocked at the idea, but unable to reverse his and Julia's lie, decided to make it sound like a good idea. "I will speak to the realtor today." He smiled, kissing her full on the mouth.

"No, no, I insist on making this my next step back to my old self," Jess sounded excited for the first time since her return home.

Unable to find the right words, "That's a good idea!" Sebastian replied, thinking why in hell didn't he protest, explaining it had been sold. "If you're sure you are up to it?" He smiled instead.

He did not want to risk seeing Jess's look of disappointment after all the time she spent confused following her treatment and trying hard to get better for him and Prissy. "I will help all I can," he added, wondering how her family would react.

"Julia, we have a problem with Jess!"

"Oh no! Is she ill again?" Julia replied, sounding panicked.

Hearing her distress, Sebastian lost no time in making it clear, "Sorry, Julia. No, she wants to make amends to her family. I stupidly lied that they were happy to help with getting her treatment."

Julia wanted to cry. "It didn't help my explaining why they had to leave their old cottage," she replied, unable to imagine the outcome.

"She's on the phone to the realtor as we speak," he added, feeling sick.

Thinking on her feet, "It will take time. Maybe we will think of something in the meantime," Julia added, but with no idea how.

"Let's make it the longest project ever," Sebastian replied with a sigh.

"I've done it," a look of glee in her eyes, Jess was ecstatic. "I'll get Chris to organise the restoration. I have many ideas of how it should look. It's not a bad cottage. An upstairs extension over the garage providing a fourth bedroom, a second shower room and outwards on the ground floor, only slightly encroaching on the large garden, will accommodate an excellent kitchen." Jess stopped before adding, "I will get them a car to leave in the garage." Her beaming smile melted Sebastian's heart.

"I'm sure they'll love it," he replied tongue in cheek.

Having caught up with Julia busying herself arranging flowers, Sebastian filled her in on Jess's plan. "It's not as if she skimped on the price she paid for the hovel. She's now intending to make it into a palace complete with a car in the garage," he rubbed the top of his head, feeling stressed.

"Dragging the build out will only extend the agony. Is there nothing you can say to her father to prepare him?" Julia stumbled over the words, realising it most unlikely.

Sebastian was hoping for a miracle. "Like what exactly?" he replied, wishing the whole thing would go away.

"Tell Jess they left shortly after he signed her consent and you have no idea where they are!" Julia added, trying desperately to come up with an idea.

"Her first port of call would be to the same guy we encountered at the municipal and I don't think I can bribe him enough not to tell her where they've gone once she explains why."

"Fair point. There must be a list of many who would kill for that crap apartment. It's a win, win for him. Oust the moron and get bribed by the next in line."

A thinking-cap the size of a giant was needed. "Chris, can I speak to you? I have a quandary," Sebastian asked.

"If it's about Jess's new project, you're too slow. She's already given me chapter and verse as to the details and I've begun to make the arrangements. Why, what's the problem?"

"Not a problem in the practical sense. I need to explain to her parents the reason for her change of heart."

"You mean they still think she's 'a waste of space', their word's not mine. When I tried a previous reconciliation on her behalf, they threw me out." Chris shocked him with the revelation.

"I had no idea she had tried before. No wonder she's convinced they still love her." Sebastian shook his head. Thanking him, he made for the bar.

Feeling tipsy, his return to Jess made matters worse. Flinging her arms around him, kissing him passionately for the first time since her recovery, "I love you with all my heart," Jess declared, opening her negligée showing a slim, firm figure with nothing hidden. In an instant, his trousers tightened.

Undoing the offending zip, Jess knelt at his feet. Stroking and kissing, all thought of her parents left his head.

As if the past months hadn't happened, Jess, as eager to please as any time in their relationship, lifted his shirt and gripping his firm cheeks, she pulled him close.

Wanting to spend more time creating the perfect storm of passion for Jess, he held her still. "Whoa!" he begged, "Let me love you more. I want both of us to be pleasured in equal measure," his kisses reached from her neck down. It took all his resolve to hold back as Jess sighed.

The impact of their surrender was off the scale. A coming together of souls totally committed to each other's pleasure was performed with tenderness and a strength unknown before.

Lying, their arms around each other, no words were spoken as the intense ardour of the moment left them speechless.

Wiping perspiration from his brow, Jess finally found the strength to raise above him. Touching him, Sebastian was unable to resist. Gently leaning back, taking the full impact of her beautiful man full of youth and vigour, Jess took the lead.

It was as if their bodies understood the other's, their passion began all over again. Sebastian's back against the bed, he was captivated by Jess as the final measure of their love was savoured with every movement.

"Well, did she concede?" Chris asked, wondering if Sebastian had found a way to deter her from the project.

The words Sebastian wanted to say were, "She conceded all right and how," and would have been one way to explain his exhaustion. "She spoke of nothing but her project. You know what she's like when she has the bit between her teeth!" Sebastian certainly did with their last lovemaking up there with the space project.

"Yes, when she's fired up, you can't get a word in edgewise," Chris hit the nail on the head, although on a different wavelength.

Trying hard to think of a solution to the dilemma of the restored cottage and how to reconcile Jess with her father before she made a fool of herself was a monumental headache.

As soon as her father set his eyes on Jess, she would know Sebastian lied and her father was still the same miserable b… she had once considered him to be.

This could set her back mentally, Sebastian mulled, having no idea what to do. Sitting down with Julia and Chris, they began brainstorming. "What if…?" Julia began, then stopped. Knowing Jess's father, he would no sooner back down than fly in the air. She shook her head in despair.

"Come clean!" Chris said matter-of-factly.

"I had considered that, but I fear the outcome, should Jess feel let down again." Sebastian, beside himself, spent the rest of the morning deliberating.

It was when he paid a visit to the brothel that he had an idea. Seeing the chief inspector alighting the stairs, having spent the afternoon being entertained by one of their girls, it occurred to him.

Making sure his plan was viable, her family still in the same apartment, her sisters in Europe for the time being, it was all systems go.

"Excuse me, Chief Inspector, I wonder if you could help me? It seems Jess's father has been accused of abusing his family. It's not true, of course, it's just someone trying to blackmail him."

"How can I help?" Basil asked his friends, anxious to join his next chosen partner for the evening.

"Well, it's like this!"

The story told by Sebastian was a total lie. Having devised what he considered a fool proof plan, the pair sat in the grand hall drinking whisky over ice.

Coughing, feeling slightly embarrassed, Sebastian began, "Jess's father is being blackmailed. A scallywag cousin of Jess's is short of money and has threatened to expose him as an abuser of his daughters, for goodness sake. It's all a lie, of course, but I wondered if you would pretend to arrest her father and question him with the intention of drawing her cousin out as the blackmailer.

"The latter plan is for you to speak to Jess as one of the victims." Sebastian hastily added, "Her father needs to think it's real for our purpose. We know the cousin is the blackmailer and want to scare the wits out of him." He hoped to make it sound authentic.

Having patiently listened, Basil the inspector replied, "It would have to be on the QT, you understand. It would be unprofessional for me to not take the correct action in such a case," Basil answered, drawn between his professional self and his behind the curtain sexual pleasures.

"The idea is to prevent him playing such tricks again and before he gets into more trouble. He's a live wire with ideas above his station. If I can stop him now before he does real damage, it will help keep him out of jail later. Prevention being better than a cure!" Sebastian subtly using Basil's visits to their brothel as leverage.

Having thought through the idea, "It seems reasonable when you explain it in those terms. When would you like me to pay her father a visit?"

"As soon as possible, say next week!" Sebastian tried to read his thoughts.

The project almost complete, Sebastian did not want Jess to storm around, handing her father the key. "Would you convince him you will contact Jess as a witness to his innocence, not mentioning her cousin?"

"Unconventional, but if you think it will help keep that scallywag on the straight and narrow, I'll give it a try." The inspector, warming to the idea of stopping a serial offender, agreed.

Sebastian called on Julia and Chris, having explained Basil's acceptance to the first part of his plan. "For the next part, I will write a statement supposedly from Jess, confirming his innocence to the abuse lie. My thinking is," Sebastian took a breath, "when they consider each other to be their saviour, Jess's father for signing the consent to her treatment and Jess for standing as witness to his innocence of abuse, they will be reconciled and the cottage Jess has restored for them will be accepted graciously."

"There's a lot of supposition in all the subterfuge," Julia said, having paid attention to his spiel.

"Basil can be very convincing as well you know. He has convinced his wife he's faithful for many years." Sebastian smiled a mischievous smile.

"Let's hope no one discovers your tomfoolery," Julia replied, secretly admiring his tenacity.

The scene was set and Basil read Jess's father his Miranda rights. "I am arresting you for abusing one or all of your daughters." Basil hesitated. "You have the right to remain silent. Anything you say can and will be used against you in a court of law. You have the right to an attorney." He began making notes, awaiting her father's comments, but none were forthcoming.

Sitting speechless for a moment, Jess's father shook his head. "This is a joke?" he questioned, followed by, "Get out now, if you know what's good for you." He hollered, as a rooky officer took hold of his arms and fastened the handcuffs.

Back at the station and as instructed, Basil discharged the rooky officer and began his script. "Let me see, you have three daughters. We will need testimony as to your denial."

"It's a set up. My two daughters are away!" Jess's father protested, ignoring Jess as his youngest.

"Then we must proceed with the assumption you're guilty as charged until they get back!" Basil began to leave the holding room. Turning, he gave the body blow, "It says here you have three daughters. I will approach the one still here? Let me see, she lives at…" The inspector read aloud Jess's address.

"It's no good asking her to stand up for me. We don't speak," he added, looking down in the mouth. "Who said I did it? It's a lie," he continued, unable to believe the unfolding saga.

Ignoring the question, "I'll get my sergeant to call on her and see what she has to say." Basil walked from the room.

Shouting after him, "You're wasting your time!" Jess's father despaired.

It's all going to plan, Basil smiled to himself, rubbing his hands together, enjoying the pretence. Had it been real, it would have been a different story.

Chapter Thirty-Two

Waiting impatiently for the outcome, Sebastian and Julia sat mulling over the consequences.

A catastrophe on an insurmountable scale should the inspector fail, elation for Jess and onward contentment should he succeed. There was no going back and the result was in the balance.

Sitting upright, bracing themselves for the worst, the pair were unable to speak. Smiling as he entered, it was difficult to imagine how Jess's father had behaved.

Relaying the ongoing saga, Basil explained, "I have only one issue regarding the plan. I had to hold him overnight, as he wouldn't confirm I speak with Jess," he smiled. "Whatever the problem, he was prepared to stay in a cell overnight rather than allow me to consult with her."

"Serves him right for the way he's treated Jess," Sebastian, beyond relieved, grinned and turned to Basil, adding, "We will be forever in your debt." He sighed, handing him Jess's so-called assurance of her father's innocence.

Not exactly a glowing reference, but one that clearly exonerated him from the accusation. "I hope it's worded correctly."

Chis had stealthily placed the letter between others to get Jess's signature and Sebastian was satisfied the next part of plan would work.

Securing the letter in his inside pocket, Basil made his way upstairs for a free 'night on the tiles'.

"We can only wait and see!" Sebastian confirmed as the three stood with bated breath for the outcome.

"Let's hope Jess and her dad don't get their heads together regarding the detail," Chris said, forever the pessimist.

"I'll make sure they're not alone for the reconciliation. I think if we arrange a car to collect her family, I will escort Jess to the cottage while you and Chris show them around." He looked toward Julia. "I'm sure between us we can make sure her father's never left alone with Jess." Both Chris and Julia held up crossed fingers.

"I think he swallowed it," Basil confirmed. "He and his wife were extremely grateful to Jess for confirming nothing untoward happened. I'm sure I saw a tear in her father's eye as they left the station. Her mother wept, asking me to thank her. I even suggested they let bygones be bygones." His smile broad, thinking of more freebies at the brothel.

Feeling relief wash over him, Sebastian found Jess. "Come here and give me a kiss," he whispered, hoping for more.

Taking his hand having kissed his neck, "I have a surprise for you!" Jess grinned. Instead of the bed, Jess moved towards the stairs.

Quickening her steps, she opened the door. Sandy placed his cap on his head, giving a pretend salute. "Your car awaits," he smiled a knowing smile.

"It's too early for lunch. I had visions of taking advantage of you," Sebastian whispered as she guided him into the rear seat. "In the back of the car?" he laughed. "And with Sandy watching. I don't think so!"

"Later," a gruff voice and a sexy lift of the skirt, Jess joked. "Home, James, and don't spare the horses."

It was obvious Sandy was in the picture as he left the mansion at haste and turned onto the main thoroughfare. "It's a secret," Jess looked under her eyes, taunting Sebastian unashamedly.

"Stop now, you're killing me," he sat uncomfortably in the luxury of cream leather seats.

As soon as they turned the corner, Sebastian knew exactly where they were, "It's finished!" A struggle between shock and anticipation, he hesitated.

Jess whooped as she handed him the key to her family's fully restored home.

Although still a nagging concern, Sebastian had to admit, "It's wonderful, Jess. I wouldn't have recognised it from the pictures." He was about to say, "When I last saw it," but quickly changed his answer.

"I knew you'd like it. They've made a splendid job." Her happiness took all his negativity away.

"Let's christen it," Sebastian said. Unable to contain his passion a moment longer, they fell onto the king size bed.

"Do you think Father will mind?" Jess laughed as another milestone in her life began.

"Mind? I think he would be happy for you," Sebastian lied, hopefully for the last time.

***

"Now, how do we tell him?" Chris questioned. "I think a visit with a handing over the keys ceremony and a bottle of his favourite."

"I have no idea what his favourite is. Probably anything alcoholic in a bottle," Julia replied, thinking of their encounter when the odour of his breath spoke for itself.

"Personally, I don't want to see the moron again, so my thoughts were, Jess send the keys with a letter explaining her reasoning and thanking him. That way, no slip ups regarding our lies."

Just as the conversation abated, Jess appeared. "I have a brilliant idea!"

Sebastian's heart dropped. "Not another idea that needs everyone to rectify the fallout," he whispered to Julia.

No one spoke. "Well, aren't you going to ask what it is?" Jess looked from one to the other and back.

Sebastian stepped forward and hugged her, "Of course, darling, we can't wait!" A sideways glance as Julia cringed and Chris grimaced.

"I will send Sandy to collect them in the limo and we can wait at the door with the key as a surprise. What do you think?" she almost squealed with enthusiasm.

"Wonderful," Sebastian cajoled.

"Great idea," Julia smiled.

"Why didn't we think of that?" Chris gushed, squeezing her hand.

"That's settled," Jess looked satisfied as Sebastian looked like a rabbit in headlights. Chris grinned like a Cheshire cat and Julia pretend sneezed, unable to think of anything coherent, nodded her head.

Jess danced out of the room convinced she had it sewn up.

"Maybe she's right! At least they won't meet up on their own and give the show away!" Julia reasoned.

The day of judgment crept closer, doing nothing for Sebastian's anxiety. "What if they hate it?" he spoke quietly on the phone to Julia.

"Damage limitation. I'm sure you'll think of something."

"My brain aches with thinking," Sebastian took a deep breath. "I just don't want Jess back to where she was. I think I will kill him on the spot it he fouls up."

"You'll have to crawl over me to get to the moron," Julia murmured. "Although there may be no need. One day at a time." She added, "Not long now!"

Breezing in, Jess spun around. "What do you think? Will this look be ok?"

"Darling, you look stunning. How could anything not be ok on that figure?" Sebastian, overwhelmed by her beauty, felt his emotion rise.

"I want this to be perfect. At last, my family will be together after all these years," Jess looked radiant.

Sebastian's heart bled for the girl and woman that had so much love to give if only she'd been given a chance.

Suddenly, his thoughts changed, *I may never have met her had she enjoyed a normal life.* His anxiety melted as gratitude for all they had shared filled his mind.

I won't let him spoil what we have, he said to himself as Jess kissed him full on the mouth. Their tongues met and the temptation to remove the clothes she had carefully chosen was overwhelming, as was his longing to make love to the love of his life.

Careful to not crumple her, he put his hand on her breast. "I'll show you what true love means when we get back," he promised, breathing heavily, wishing the day was ended and his passion satisfied.

Cupping his face with her hands, Jess sighed, "You tease. You know we must wait!" It was almost impossible to draw herself away as his passion was obvious.

"The time has come!" Jess smiled toward Julia, who looked almost as stunning.

"We're with you all the way," she replied, taking in the radiance Jess displayed.

Adjusting his tie, Chris opened the car door. "After you, madam!" He extenuated his attitude towards the limousine, which sparkled almost as much as Jess.

Sebastian held Jess's hand, feeling a trembling the occasion had inspired. Kissing her gently, he smiled. "One step at a time, darling," he cajoled, knowing they would get through it together.

Not exactly as they expected, Jess's father hadn't bothered to change. His scruffy jacket, the one hanging on the door when they visited his apartment, was added to by filthy jeans and shoes that had seen better days.

At least her mother and sisters had tried, looking suitably attired. The parties came together, not running forward and hugging. *A more measured effort,* Sebastian thought, wondering what next as Jess and her father faced each other for the first time in an age.

The first words from her father, "What's this all about?" He was scowling, thinking it a cruel joke as their previous house was sold.

Ignoring his posturing, "Nice to see you!" her mother smiled as her sisters stepped forward with a welcoming hug.

"We've missed you," they chorused, which brought a tear to Jess's eyes.

Turning to her father, she said, "It's all yours," gesticulating to the magic she had created. "With my love and thanks," she added with a smile.

Sebastian cringed. The word 'thanks' resonated as his lie laid bare.

"Come here, girl. I'm also very grateful," her father took his elegant daughter in his arms.

It was all Julia could do not to throw up as Sebastian adlibbed. "Yes," he replied in haste before the crap hit the fan. "Jess also thanks you for your kindness," skipping the abuse case that never was.

Jess indicated the cottage and handed him the keys. "I hope you will be happy here," she added, breaking Sebastian's heart, knowing the truth.

"And this," Julia passed him the bottle of champagne, hoping to distract further conversation.

Turning to her mom, Jess added, "I hope you like it?"

Jumping up and down, her sisters were ecstatic. "You did this for us?" they shouted as her father put the key in the door with a shaky hand.

"What have you done to the old place? Have you bought it?" he seemed lost for words.

"That's a first," Sebastian whispered to Julia. "He usually has more than his share to say."

"It's in your name," Jess replied, looking delighted, wanting him to hug her. A step too far too soon.

Her sisters ran up the stairs, "Which one is our bedroom?" they squealed with joy.

Julia took charge of the detail. "You have one each," she laughed, seeing how happy they were.

Jess sat in the lounge with her mom. "I hope it makes up for the past?" Jess spoke softly, holding her mom's hand for the first time since she left home.

"It's lovely. I'm not sure what we did to deserve it. It wasn't your fault the family broke up."

"I had ambitions above my station, as I recall. But it's worked out well in the end."

A tear in her eye, she sat close to her mom, who placed a loving arm around her shoulder. "He's a stubborn man. Many old-fashioned ideas where girls are concerned. Don't speak until spoken to, being just one, and as you know, you were well versed in speaking your mind." She smiled.

"True, it's my intention to clean the slate," Jess murmured as the door flew open.

"Have you seen in the garage?" Pamela, the youngest, screamed.

Unable to believe her eyes, "Is it really ours?" Margarita added, clapping her hands together.

"Yes, of course. Do you drive?" Jess asked, realising her dad had lost his licence through drink many years ago.

"We both do. I can't wait to try it!" Pam said, flinging her arms around Jess.

All's going well, Sebastian thought, wiping sweat from his brow for the umpteenth time. "So far, so good," he whispered to Julia.

The invitation to the wedding was next, "I hope you can make it, Mom?" Awaiting a reply, Jess added,

"There's a little something to help with the upkeep of the house and to get you back on your feet."

A check for $100,000 was stared at in disbelief. Seeing the shock on her mom's face, Jess added quickly, "It's fine. I am more than able to cover the costs. Tell Dad not to worry."

Fingers crossed they would attend her wedding. Jess turned to leave with a smile.

Opening the limo door with enthusiasm, Sebastian and Julia waved with relief.

Chapter Thirty-Three

Once the celebration for a job well done and the keys were handed over without consequence, Sebastian reminisced. Thinking of the past, present and what was to come, a wedding so spectacular and costly it made his eyes water, he was grateful to have only a small part to play. The words 'I do' the most important.

Prissy paraded the umpteenth flower-girl dress. "Well, what do you think? Isn't this the best yet?" she asked the same question of each beautiful offering. She was right, of course. Sharing her mother's good looks, pale complexion and magnificent eyes, how could he not be captivated?

Sebastian smiled, prouder than ever of his kind and gentle, not forgetting beautiful, daughter. "They're all wonderful, darling."

Everyone pulled out the stops, including Howard with the garden, fairy lights emblazoned in the trees as darkness fell, the pool cleaned to perfection, and floating candles the highlight around the fountain.

Evening had been Jess's choice for the ceremony. "It seems more romantic somehow," Jess had convinced Sebastian, although at rehearsal, the justice of the peace had difficulty reading the script.

"How can it not be wonderful with you there? I'm sure it will be perfect," Sebastian reassured her.

Although Jess laughed, pointing out they had been man and wife in real terms from just after they met, he was still a romantic.

"I love you so!" she whispered. "Now go away and let me concentrate," she added, seeing a familiar look in his eye.

"Personally, I can't wait to consummate our relationship," Sebastian grinned. "Again and again and again," he added, reaching out, holding a kiss that took her breath away.

Sandy polished the cars to perfection. His outfit as head chauffeur was dark blue with a cream cravat, matching Chris's as best man.

The small but select guests would be ferried to the church and afterwards to the small mansion. No mention of the brothel was allowed.

Chris checked the stables. Every detail of the bridal procession must be perfect. The horses were brushed, dressed in flowers and bows matching the bride's gown. Uniforms for the riders and staff, were pristine in black and white, not forgetting the dogs. Deisel looking splendid in his black and white spotted dicky-bow and Jeremy in matching waistcoat. It was set to be the wedding, not only of the year, but the century.

Nothing was spared. Coach and white horses to carry the bride to the church with her father, hopefully, if he stayed sober. Champagne fountains, a three-foot high wedding cake extravaganza, delicacies from all over the world set out by the chefs, the lavish spread compared only to the White House when foreign allies were invited.

Keeping their brothel out of sight, nothing was left to chance. Guards, although present, were invisible. No one was allowed through the now boarded up gate at the end of the garden. Orders carried out should any guest ask what lie behind, "It's a nunnery, no admission," was to be the mantra instructed.

As the day drew nearer, nerves were heightened. "I wasn't this anxious when Prissy was born," Jess said, feeling the tension of families meeting up for the first time.

Their backgrounds like chalk and cheese, Jess hoped her father had changed his socks. "Not unusual for him to dress up and forget the niceties," Jess recalled. "It was only at funerals he tried and then he had to be checked for mismatched or overlooked garments."

A frown appeared, a first for Jess in a while. Only since he accepted his role of 'father of the bride', when the excitement of the day found Jess forgetting her upbringing, did she consider the outcome.

"Don't worry," Chris smiled. "I've sent outfits for them all. I took your sister to the mall and she guided me. She's a sweetheart!" he added with affection. Had he not been gay, Jess would have thought him interested emotionally.

"What would I do without you?" Jess kissed his cheek.

"You won't have to. I'm a stayer!" he laughed. After so many years, Jess didn't doubt it.

"A day to remember for the rest of your life!" was how Julia phrased it, as Jess seemed distracted.

"I hope you're right," apprehension slipping in between the excitement. "They haven't met yet!" Jess said, thinking how different from his family her family was.

Nerves abounded as the guests arrived. "These are my parents," Jess smiled, introducing them to Sebastian's family for the first time.

Holding her breath, Jess's father surprised her. Nodding, he held out his hand.

She took it willingly, saying, "Pleased to meet you." Sebastian's father smiled, looking toward his wife for confirmation his actions were acceptable.

Jess's mother intervened, expecting some wisecrack from her belligerent husband. "Likewise, I'm sure," she spoke for them both.

Sebastian's mother finally looked up. "I'm Mrs Bryce-Parks," she smiled a forced smile, obviously prepared with her pale green gloves and matching designer outfit complete with a small but perfectly placed fascinator.

Prissy didn't help as she stepped up, "Oh, you have the same name as my daddy and me!" Out of the mouths of babes!!!!

The reply came without a second breath, "Oh, do we?" Sebastian's mother replied, quick off the mark, taking a closer look.

"Yes, I'm Priscilla Bryce-Parks, but you can call me Prissy." Cat out of the bag, big style!

"Well, Julia, what do you think?" Jess asked, hiding in the toilet until the dust had settled.

"They'll have to suck it up," Julia replied, thinking of their outdated attitude to babies before weddings.

Checking their makeup and putting on a pretend smile, the pair made for the dining hall. "It's time for practice dancing," Jess announced, nodding to the leader of the band. Taking Sebastian by surprise, Jess tapped his shoulder from behind. "Care to dance, handsome?" she questioned, holding out her arms.

"She knows!" was all Sebastian could muster.

Holding him close as they began to waltz, "I know she knows!" Jess answered through gritted teeth. "Well, did you get the third degree?"

"Not exactly, but she made me promise not to mention our 'promiscuous oversight' if we visit England."

"Promiscuous oversight!" Jess laughed out loud. "More an out-of-control f..., if you ask me," Jess replied behind her hand. "I remember it well!" she continued to smirk.

"Jess, you're a caution. What will I do with you?" Sebastian hesitated. "You know how strait-laced Mom is!"

"When we go to bed, I'll show you what to do with me!" she grinned sexily, sounding if not looking like a brothel keeper.

The encounter on the back burner, the pair greeted their guests as Chris guided them to their seats. As requested, their families were seated as far away from each other as possible.

Served on silver platters, the food was exceptional. Butlers poured wine into crystal goblets with the instructions to keep Jess's father's alcoholic beverages to a minimum.

Congratulating the caterers and staff for their excellent participation, Sebastian and Jess considered their wedding feast everything they had hoped for.

Chris's speech was funny but measured, as instructed. No smut or inappropriate jokes and no mention of Jess and Julia's business acumen.

Looking around, it seemed a million light years away from the brothel with its bawdy jokes and sexual inuendo. *What would his mother think if she knew?* Jess asked herself, seeing her making small talk with dignitaries sworn to secrecy regarding their indiscretions.

Whispering, she turned to Julia. "I hope she never discovers our profession," Jess smirked, watching his mother move through the guests, recognising upper echelon for preference to chat to.

"I hope Prissy isn't aware of what we do for a living. She has a knack of letting the cat out of the bag." Julia laughed, thinking of the 'you have the same name as me' revelation.

The grand hall was dressed in an array of seasonal flowers carefully collected by Howard's helpers and suitably arranged by the wedding planners.

A Glenn Miller sounding orchestra played a variety of music to dance to. The waltz, quickstep and jive ended the night with a rock and roll band. "To suit everyone's taste," as requested, a broad smile on Jess's face.

Keeping one eye on her father, hoping he wouldn't begin his version of 'in the mood' (or was that 'nude'?) and the other eye on Sebastian's parents, hoping it was to their taste, Jess was exhausted.

When the orchestra struck up 'Moonlight Serenade', Sebastian took his new wife in his arms. "My God, you're beautiful! How did I get so lucky?" He held her tight.

The warmth of Sebastian's body, his skill on the dancefloor almost equal to his skill in bed, Jess eagerly awaited their honeymoon.

Lost in the moment, their guests faded. "I'm the lucky one," Jess whispered, his fragrance irresistible as their bodies danced as one.

Looking around for Sebastian's parents for the millionth time, Jess was shocked to find his mom waltzing with Prissy. "You look lovely," Prissy was heard saying as his dad joined in for a threesome.

With Prissy in his arms as they danced, "I love your daughter," his mom murmured to Jess.

Sebastian, holding his breath, wondered, '*What next!* "Yes, your granddaughter is rather special," Jess grinned like a Cheshire cat.

A sigh of relief as his mom smiled back, his beaming face said it all, "My Queen of Tarts, it looks like our Prissy takes after you!" Sebastian laughed. "You always manage a quick retort." He kissed Jess full on the mouth.

"A toast to the bride and groom," glasses raised, the day had been perfect. Chris, their best man, smiled. "To the happy couple." The congregation joined in as the band played 'Congratulations'.

A day befitting the endearing love Jess and Sebastian shared had been the happiest day of all. "One to remember for the rest of our lives," Jess romanced.

Slipping away to change for their honeymoon with anticipation and excitement, this had been destined from the moment they met.

An exchange of glances, two beating hearts unable to control their passion, the excuse to be together for the first time as man and wife proved irresistible.

Lifting his new wife in his arms, they entered their bedroom. The flower-strewn stately four-poster bed dressed in white satin for the occasion, all thoughts of their family and guests disappeared as Sebastian laid her down gently. "I love you so much it hurts," Sebastian murmured as he skilfully unzipped her white satin gown. Nothing now stood in their way.

Jess's family together despite their differences, Sebastian's family's love for Prissy set in stone, it was a befitting start to their married life.

No need for fancy words. Their held eye contact was all it took to ignite his arousal. Jess stood before him, wife, lover and exclusive sexual partner forever. He intended to express his feelings with all the passion he possessed.

"Wow," slipped from Jess's lips as they lay sated in each other's arms.

"Wow, indeed," Sebastian's reaction to the best lovemaking ever was sealed with a gentle, "Never doubt me again." The phone rang, breaking the magic.

"Your limousine is here. Are you ready?" Chris's voice sounded cautiously urgent.

"We'll be down. Just give us a minute." Sebastian grinned, pulling on his trousers as Jess rushed to the shower. "I better not join you, or it will be tomorrow before we go on honeymoon."

Composing themselves for the grand entrance, the groom dressed to kill in a grey silk suit and the bride's outfit in burgundy and cream, befitting a princess. They closed the door to the bedroom and approached the grand staircase.

Causing a sensation, Jess hesitated. Turning, she lifted her bouquet, tossing it into the air, hoping Julia would be first to grasp it. She closed her eyes.

It was her dearest wish that her friend would feel for a man the way she felt for Sebastian. *Maybe one day,* she held her breath as the bouquet sailed up in the air and into her sister Margarita's hands.

"Not another stupid fool in the family!" her father shouted, shaking his head. If Jess didn't know better, she thought there was a smile on his face.

"Where have you been?" Prissy stepped forward looking beautiful in her bridesmaid's dress, spring flowers still in her hair.

"Getting ready for our honeymoon. We'll be back soon," Sebastian added, lifting her high, not wanting her to worry whilst they were away.

Hugging his neck and a kiss on the cheek, "I know about honeymoons," she giggled, looking adorable.

"I hope not!" Sebastian whispered, a sideways glance and a smile towards his new wife.

The confetti and rose petals thrown in the air by their nearest and dearest were the icing on the wedding cake.

An island paradise awaiting, the pair put the past behind them. A beautiful hotel overlooking a warm sea with sunsets to die for, Hawaii had it all.

They turned to wave, seeing their happiness shared by their families. Prissy waving her posy, Julia looking emotional and Chris and Howard grinning from ear to ear. Two people in love, this was set to be the honeymoon to end all honeymoons.

"Mummy, you look beautiful," Prissy said, arms around her neck.

Jess reflected, thinking back to her mousey hair, protruding teeth, dark-rimmed spectacles and empty pockets. Her journey had been worthwhile!